NO STONE UNTURNED

Patricia Robins

CHIVERS

British Library Cataloguing in Publication Data available

This Large Print edition published by BBC Audiobooks Ltd, Bath, 2010.
Published by arrangement with the Author.

U.K. Hardcover ISBN 978 1 408 45744 3
U.K. Softcover ISBN 978 1 408 45745 0

Printed and bound in Great Britain by CPI Antony Rowe, Chippenham
and Eastbourne

NO STONE UNTURNED

ONE

The bell rang and the art room exploded into its customary end-of-lesson noise. Paintings were stacked against the walls to dry; brushes put away in the cupboards; easels stacked, paint water thrown down the sink. Girls and boys jostled one another, laughing, chattering in subdued voices. Soon they would be making considerably more noise as they left the big new Comprehensive school building and crowded on to buses or rode their bikes or walked home. For the moment, they were still reasonably controlled.

Sandra White surveyed the groups of departing children with a mixture of relief and affection. It was good to know that another weekend had arrived and there would be freedom for her, too, until Monday morning. Yet she loved her work and as art mistress to the senior pupils, she was in a privileged place. Art was only compulsory in the primary classes. These fourteen, fifteen, sixteen-year-olds were voluntarily taking O' levels and were therefore enthusiastic and very little trouble to manage, despite the fact that she was only five years older than some of her students.

The studio emptied rapidly. Soon only one child was left—a thin, dark-eyed, rather attractive girl called Julia Forbes. For a moment Sandra could not remember if the child was fourteen or fifteen. She was a promising artist and her drawings and paintings were imaginative and sensitive.

The girl approached the dais where Sandra was standing with slow uncertain steps. She liked the young art teacher and to a certain extent, tried to emulate her cool poised manner, her soft attractive voice; even the short and wavy cut of her chestnut brown hair, and the way she made up her eyes. But this Friday afternoon, miserable, frightened and desperate, Julia's manner was far from poised. She was on the verge of tears as she whispered:

'Can I speak to you, please, Miss White?'

Sandra's blue eyes looked briefly into Julia's brown ones. She saw at once that the girl was about to cry.

'Of course, Julia!' she said gently, stepping down off the platform and putting an arm round the girl's shoulders. 'What's the trouble?'

'Oh, Miss White . . . !' The tears came now—deep convulsive childish sobs. Sandra let her cry for a moment and then said:

'Come along now, Julia. Nothing can be as bad as all that. Whatever is wrong, I'm sure we can put it right. What *is* wrong?'

It was not unusual in a huge Comprehensive school such as this one which served Ashwyck

2

and the surrounding villages, for an occasional teenage girl to become pregnant. When Sandra had come to the school a year ago, the headmistress had warned her to expect such events from time to time and, of course, to report such matters to her. Though she was not shocked, therefore, to learn that a mere fifteen-year-old could be in this kind of trouble, Sandra was astonished that it should be young Julia Forbes. The girl was serious, intelligent and, she would have judged, anything but promiscuous. The only child of parents somewhat older than most, Julia had always seemed to take school, her work, her O' levels and life generally very seriously.

As Julia sobbed, Sandra tried to search her memory for her mental card index on her pupils. As far as she could recall, Julia had a steady relationship with that tall, thin scholarly boy in the upper sixth—Tony Dodd.

'Julia, is it Tony?' she asked carefully.

Julia broke into a fresh storm of weeping. Gradually, Sandra elicited the facts. Although Julia and the boy imagined themselves in love, nothing 'wrong' had ever taken place. Tony wasn't like that—he respected her; understood her wish to stay a virgin. No, it wouldn't be so awful if it had been Tony . . .

Sandra was shocked now by the pathetic little story which followed. It seemed that Julia and Tony had gone to a rock concert to listen to a new band which went by the name of The Handle. One of the band was an eighteen-year-old boy called Mike Shaw—the lead guitarist. Somehow—Sandra wasn't quite able to ascertain how—the boy had noticed Julia and asked her to join him in the interval for a drink. Tony Dodd had gone home in a huff because Julia, not unnaturally flattered to be noticed by the Shaw boy, had accepted his invitation. There was, therefore, no Tony to take Julia home at the end of the dance. Mike, who had a car, offered to drive her home. On the way he had stopped on the Common and despite Julia's protests, had dragged her into a clump of bushes. Julia had been terrified but instead of screaming, had tried to talk the boy into leaving her alone. She had fought against him but he paid no attention to her tearful resistance and it was over in a few minutes.

All this had happened six weeks ago. Julia had tried to forget all about it. The band left Ashwyck next day and she never expected to see the boy again. She hadn't told anyone—least of all Tony or her parents—what had happened. Now she had to speak of it because she suspected she was pregnant. She knew she could trust Sandra—could Sandra please help.

Sandra did what she could to comfort and reassure the child. She was appalled. From Julia's account—and she did not doubt the girl's word—it was a clear case of rape, though whether this could be proved she very much doubted. Obviously there were no witnesses and the boy, Mike Shaw, could easily deny Julia's story or say she had been a willing participant.

She, Sandra, would have to report the whole story to Mrs Sinclair, the headmistress. Meanwhile she suggested to Julia that she somehow found the courage to tell her parents. They would have to know.

'I can't, Miss, I can't! You don't know my dad. He'd kill me. Mum, too. You see, I'm all they've got. They've been counting on me doing well at school and getting to university. They want me to be a teacher. The disgrace would kill them . . .'

Sandra sighed. Vaguely she recalled the girl's parents. Mr Forbes had a large newspaper and sweet shop in the village. Mrs Forbes helped him run it. They were enormously ambitious for their daughter and obviously idolised her. Sandra knew from other members of the staff that there was a certain amount of pressure put on the girl by her father; too much pressure. The girl was nervy and if anything, over-studious.

She sent Julia home, telling her she would think about her problem overnight. Julia could come to her flat next morning for coffee and maybe by then Sandra would have worked something out.

As Sandra walked home the problem of

5

Julia was very much on her mind. Perhaps, she told herself, Rudge would be able to make some helpful suggestions. She was meeting him at six o'clock.

Bob Rudgely was a reporter on the local paper, the *Stanfield Observer.* He'd only come to Ashwyck six months ago and was living at the Waterman's Arms, the old Tudor pub in the village. Since meeting him whilst out walking on the golf course soon after his arrival at Ashwyck, Sandra and he had become constant companions.

Rudge was twenty-seven. He was a large, rather untidy young man with fair hair and grey-green eyes which were nearly always full of laughter. He had enormous charm and Sandra, who began by liking him, had now reached the point where she was three parts in love with him. Rudge seemed to be of the same mind about her. Their friendship was ripening into something deeper and more romantic but slowly, pleasantly and without the usual violent repercussions of love-at-first-sight.

Thinking about it, as she so often found herself doing nowadays, Sandra felt that this was the right way—the best way, to fall in love. She felt confident that Rudge would, when he finally made up his mind to settle down, ask her to marry him; knew that she would probably say yes. But for the moment, he wasn't completely sure he wanted to stay on the *Stanfield Observer*, or in Ashwyck, for the rest of his life. He'd set his sights on becoming a reporter for a national newspaper and yet he didn't want to have to live and work in a big city! He was essentially a country lover. He enjoyed all outdoor sports; loved golf, swimming and was a dedicated fisherman. At Ashwyck, he could do all these things. A sizeable river ran eastward through the village, the upper part of which was reserved for fishing. At the west end of the village, where the river widened, it formed a natural swimming pool. He often took Sandra there on warm days.

The golf course was only nine holes but a pretty course and not too crowded. Rudge had become a member and had initiated Sandra into the game. She was now having lessons every week with Bill Wells, the Australian golf pro and had become almost as keen on the game as Rudge himself. Rudge teased her a lot, telling her she had only really become interested since he had introduced her to Bill.

Sandra had smiled, not at all displeased because Rudge was a little jealous of the tall, blond, Australian who, she was well aware, was more than casually interested in her.

Rudge was waiting for her in the lounge of the Waterman's Arms, a half-finished beer on the table in front of him. He got to his feet and fetched her a shandy without asking her if she wanted it. He was obviously wound up and eager to impart some news to her. She decided to let him talk himself out first before she asked his advice about poor little Julia.

'Couldn't wait for you to get here, Sandie!' he burst out as soon as they were both settled at the table. His grey eyes were bright with excitement. 'I'm on to something very mysterious—at least, I think I am!'

For some weeks past he had been working on a series of articles entitled Local Beauty Spots. At weekends, Sandra had accompanied him and together they had discovered all sorts of interesting and historical facts about Ashwyck and the surrounding countryside. Rudge wrote easily and simply and his articles were seemingly well received, for his editor, having asked originally for six, decided to let Rudge go ahead and do a further half-dozen.

On the previous Wednesday, Rudge and Sandra had spent a fascinating evening in the local graveyard. Rudge had wanted to find out which was the oldest grave. The church itself dated back to Norman times and he had felt sure there must be amongst the crumbled slanting gravestones, some interesting historical record of the past. Instead, they had discovered a fairly recent grave of an unknown man.

As the sexton was not about, Rudge said he would return another day to enquire about it. He'd been too busy on Thursday, he told

Sandra, but today he'd managed to go back to the churchyard. The sexton had told him that the man's body had been found in Baker's Pool, part of the river where trout abounded. Foul play had been suspected but never proved and despite extensive enquiries, the body was never identified.

Sandra looked at Rudge's excited face, her own puzzled.

'I can't see what you can make of a story like that,' she said, as Rudge paused to draw breath and finish his beer. 'It must have been written up at the time. Who would be interested now, three years later?'

'But that's just it!' Rudge said, leaning forward and covering Sandra's hand with his own. 'After I'd heard all this from the sexton, I went back to the office to look up the old records—just out of curiosity—and, Sandie, there wasn't a single solitary item on the files.'

'But there must have been!' Sandra said. 'The papers at that time were bound to have reported the finding of the body—the inquest—even if they didn't make a splash of the story.'

'The records are incomplete!' Rudge said triumphantly. 'I went through them all, and there are gaps at the relevant times. Someone has removed copies from the files!'

He looked at Sandra's startled face and grinned.

'I told you I was on to something. I

distinctly smell a rat, Sandie, and I can't wait to tackle Newman on Monday. Unfortunately, he's gone away this weekend so I can't see him till then.'

Frank Newman was the editor of the *Stanfield Observer*—a grey-haired portly man of about sixty whom Sandra knew by sight and saw occasionally at the Golf Club. He was usually with his brother, Gerald Newman, the local M.P. and his wife Cilla. Sandra avoided them, not so much because she disliked the two men but because Cilla was the hard, brittle loud-voiced type of woman she had no time for. She was always very smart, dressed in the latest fashions, and in her way, attractive. Sandra guessed she was nearer forty than thirty but it was hard to judge her age accurately. The very blonde hair was obviously dyed, the small pointed face never without carefully applied make-up. Whenever she was in the club, her shrill county-accented voice was raised above everyone else's.

As their M.P.'s wife, and because she obviously had money and lived in the Manor House, most people in Ashwyck treated Cilla Newman as well as her husband with a certain deference. Cilla Newman obviously expected it. On one occasion she had created a scene in the pro's room because she had wanted to change the time of her lesson to Sandra's and Sandra had refused, not so much from any desire to be difficult, but because, as a teacher, she had very little spare time compared with Cilla Newman. From that moment on, the older woman had cut Sandra whenever they saw one another. Not that Sandie minded particularly. Her own life did not in any way cross the Newmans though she did realise that if and when she and Rudge were married, Frank Newman, as Rudge's employer, would play a certain part in their affairs. It could be possible that she would then come up against Cilla Newman socially . . . but that was way ahead in the future and certainly did not bother Sandra now.

What was of far greater interest to her was Cilla Newman's obvious interest in Bill Wells. Sandie often saw them drinking together in the club house. Bill was a nice, simple type of fellow, thirtyish, very Australian, good-looking, easy-going. Sandra herself liked him a great deal and knew he liked her, too. She'd twice gone out with him—once to a golf club dance and once to a New Year's Eve party but since then, on any occasion he had suggested she accompany him, she was already committed to going with Rudge. At these functions, she had been unable to avoid noticing that Bill was spending his time dancing with Cilla Newman. Even Rudge had noticed and remarked to Sandie:

'Cilla Newman had best watch her step or the village will start gossiping. She's obviously keen on Bill and when she's had a few brandies, she doesn't trouble to hide her feelings! I wonder that husband of hers doesn't complain.'

But Gerald did not appear to object to his wife's flirtation with the golf pro. Nevertheless, Sandra agreed with Rudge that as wife of their M.P., Cilla should be more discreet. The election was coming up soon and it would not do Gerald Newman any good to have the slightest breath of scandal associated with his name.

Sandra brought her thoughts back to the man opposite her. When Rudge was excited, carried away by an idea as he was at this moment, there was something very appealing about him. She could understand why he made a good journalist. He was always curious about people; about life. When he had first arrived in Ashwyck, he had complained to her that the place was too quiet, too uneventful for his taste. He did not plan to stay for long. He thought he might soon become bored with the sleepy little village. But gradually, he had become absorbed in the place. On the surface, he told Sandra, Ashwyck might appear to be half asleep but he was beginning to discover a lot went on below. Life wasn't so different here than anywhere else. And beautiful though the village was, it was by no means as dormant as he had first thought. Human beings were human, even if they did live in beautiful surroundings, he told her. Though the major part of the village retained its antiquity and old-world charm, it was rapidly becoming modernised, what with the big new Comprehensive school, the disco for teenagers, the supermarket at which only last week, two respectable housewives had been caught shop-lifting!

Sandra, remembering now that Rudge's instincts were first and foremost those of a reporter, decided to extract a promise from him not to use as news anything she told him about poor little Julia Forbes. Though the child herself was of little interest to a paper, Mike Shaw certainly would be. The Handle was already making the charts. If Julia's story was true, and Sandra did not doubt it, the affair could make national, and not just local, headlines.

When Rudge, reluctantly, had given his promise, Sandra related the pathetic little story.

'Julia is frightened to death of her parents,' she ended. 'But obviously they will have to know. And, of course, I shall have to tell Mrs Sinclair. But what is worrying me, Rudge, is the child herself. She isn't promiscuous. She's rather shy and sweet and serious—timid, I suppose you'd describe her. She's just not the type to be able to face up to the kind of ordeal that lies ahead. I know she isn't really my worry but she came to me and I do want to help if I can. But how?'

Rudge sighed.

'I can see why you swore me to secrecy. What a story! I interviewed that group when they were here. I remember Shaw—a rather nasty bit of work, I thought. You know, I can't see how this *can* be kept quiet. The girl's a minor. Shaw could do time if rape were proved.'

'Well, I don't see how anyone can prove anything!' Sandra said sensibly. 'It would be her word against his. Shaw could say she acquiesced. I'm not even sure Julia's parents would take her word for her innocence.'

'I can't say I'd vouch for that father of hers,' Rudge said thoughtfully. 'He's another nasty bit of work. He's a self-opinionated, blustering, pretentious chap . . . means to get on in the world. He was the one who made all the fuss about the supermarket opening, remember? He'd see any situation in the light of how it would affect trade. He could well be the type to want to go to court from sheer vindictiveness. Frankly, I don't think much of the girl's chances of keeping this quiet once the story breaks.'

'Rudge, we mustn't let it break. You don't know Julia as I do. And there's the other boy, Tony Dodd. It may sound silly to you when they are so young but I believe they are genuinely deeply attached to each other. What would a thing like that do to them?'

'It's a pity they are so young!' Rudge said. 'Otherwise Dodd might have married her and given the kid his name, but of course that's out of the question. They're only a couple of kids themselves.'

'I believe the truth is always the best policy—as a rule,' Sandra mused. 'But I'm not so sure in this case. Perhaps if Julia could leave Mike Shaw's name out of this, there'd be a better chance of the whole thing being handled quietly. The baby could be adopted and Julia return to school when it's all over and go on with her studies.'

Rudge shrugged his shoulders.

'I don't know the girl. Do you think she's capable of withholding Shaw's name? Everyone will put pressure on her to tell them who the father is. Personally I think it would take quite a strong character to stand up to Forbes once he made up his mind to get the facts. I suppose he does *have* to be told? What about the mother?'

'I have an idea she's entirely dominated by her husband,' Sandra said. 'If he said "turn Julia out", I think she would do so rather than face up to the man. I had the impression she was frightened of him—Julia, too.'

'Poor kid!' Rudge said softly. 'What a life! Maybe the headmistress will think up a solution. Blowed if I can! Maybe something will gestate during dinner. What about it, Sandie? Hungry?'

15

She wasn't particularly hungry but she knew that Rudge had a healthy appetite. They went in to dinner. Mrs Haycock, the licencee's wife, was a good cook and usually provided them with a tasty meal.

When they had finished the excellent steak and kidney pudding, Rudge suggested to Sandra that they took a run out in his car. The June air was soft and sweet-smelling and as Rudge pointed out, it would be lovely up on the golf course with its beautiful view over Stanfield Woods and the river running softly by in the moonlight.

Sandra forgot Julia for the moment, pushing the unpleasant thought of the child's problems to the back of her mind. It was, as Rudge had pointed out, a gorgeous evening. Rudge was holding her hand and she was no longer Miss White, senior art mistress! She was twenty-one and as susceptible as any other girl to the thought of a drive in the moonlight with an attractive young man.

As Rudge had promised, it was indeed beautiful up on the deserted golf course. Rudge found a quiet place to park the car and took Sandie in his arms. With one hand he pushed the soft chestnut hair away from her small heart-shaped face. He looked down into her wide blue eyes and sighed.

'You are almost too much of a temptation to me, Sandra White,' he said. 'I find this attractive little face of yours invading my dreams. I'm losing sleep, my girl, because of you. If this goes on, I'm going to be forced to ask you to marry me.'

'Nobody's forcing you, Rudge!' Sandra whispered, laughing.

He stopped her laughter with a long, deep kiss which left them both trembling.

'I'm in love with you!' Rudge said. 'I suppose that's hardly a surprise to you. You always seem to know exactly what I'm feeling.'

'You've never actually said you loved me before,' Sandra said, snuggling contentedly in the circle of his warm, strong arms. 'Say it again.'

'No, I won't!' Rudge said and then, sighing: 'Yes, I will. I love you, Sandie. It's a confounded nuisance. I didn't want to fall in love with anyone just now. I wanted to be able to concentrate on my career—really get down to some hard work. You distract me, woman, do you know that? Half the time when I should be thinking about what I'm writing, I'm thinking of you, of this . . .' he kissed her again . . . 'and this . . . and this . . .'

'I think of you, too,' Sandra murmured. 'In art class! I even drew your face the other day when I was day dreaming.'

Rudge grinned down at her.

'Say you love me, darling. You do, don't you?' he added, suddenly uncertain of her. 'I've sometimes asked myself if you weren't rather keen on old Bill. Answer me, Sandie!'

17

'I will, if you give me a chance!' Sandra laughed, detaching herself from his embrace. 'Now, let me consider old Bill, as you call him. I think old Bill is quite attractive. I like his eyes. He has a nice mouth, too, and . . .'

'Stop it, Sandie. Say *"I love you, Bob Rudgely—you and only you!"*'

'I think I do love you,' Sandra said, suddenly serious. 'I've thought so for some time. But I'm not completely sure, Rudge. How can anyone be *completely* sure? I worry about it sometimes. In books people always know they are in love without any shadow of a doubt.'

Rudge put his arms round her and drew her close against him.

'I think everyone has "shadows of doubts" sometimes,' he said thoughtfully. 'That is, if they are capable of reasoning at all. Love can mean so many things, can't it? And who can be sure that tomorrow and tomorrow and tomorrow one will still react to a person in the same way? We, each of us, is growing and changing a little every day, with every experience. And if we change, the other person must be changing, too. Two people who loved each other quite sincerely might suddenly discover they had grown apart.'

Sandie sighed.

'That puts in words exactly how I feel!' she said. 'It's one of the things I love about you, Rudge—that you seem to feel the same way I

18

do about most things. But if you agree love is a doubtful certainty, how can *you* be sure you love *me*?"

'Darling, because I think we are growing closer together, not further apart, each day we know each other better. I've changed this last six months and I think you have, too, but it seems to me we've been finding more and more, not less and less, in common. Six months ago I'd have laughed if anyone had told me, the confirmed bachelor, that I'd be blinking about getting married. Now it doesn't seem in the least strange or funny. I think I'd like being married to you, Sandie. I want you near me all the time. I need you to talk to. I need your companionship. I need you in other ways, too.'

'Yes!' Sandie agreed breathlessly.

Their physical need of one another was never very far beneath the surface. Lying on the edge of the river in the hot sun, she would find herself wanting to touch the smooth firm skin of Rudge's shoulder or run her fingers through his glistening wet hair; to feel his strong hands on her own body where it lay not quite touching his. Her physical awareness of him was sometimes so intense that she would catch her breath and feel her heart pounding suffocatingly with her need to be near him.

He had never tried to hide his desire for her. After the first few times he had kissed her, he had said, half teasing but with an underlying seriousness:

19

'You'll have to watch your step with me, Sandie. I have a passionate nature. Give me half a chance and I'll make love to you, my girl!'

They had both laughed and the moment passed but there were others when, as now, they were quite alone and their kissing had become more and more desperate. Then Rudge had said:

'Don't say "no" unless you really mean it, darling. When you do, I'll stop whatever I'm doing because I'll know that's as far as you want to go. It's up to you.'

But it wasn't always so easy for Sandie to say 'stop'. There were times when she had nearly given way and times when she had thought she was silly not to give way. But now that Rudge had spoken at last of marriage, she wasn't sorry. As a school teacher she couldn't afford to have even a breath of gossip attaching to her—and hiding anything in this village would be quite impossible, least of all an affair. She could almost smile at the thought of the gossip there would be if Rudge was seen leaving her flat in the early hours of the morning.

'I'll get you a ring, darling!' Rudge was saying, his lips against her mouth. 'Then that blasted golf pro will know just whose girl you really are. I love you, Sandie. I love you!'

'I love you, too!' she said, and for the moment, there was not even the shadow of a doubt.

TWO

Gerald Newman looked across the breakfast table at his wife with a mixture of fear and dislike. He found it hard to remember that once he had been madly in love with her; that the summit of happiness lay in the thought that he was married to one of the most attractive and popular girls in his set.

How long had it taken for him to wake up to the fact that Cilla had married him for his money? How long before he had discovered she was having affairs with other men? He couldn't remember. They had been married now for nearly twenty years and he'd lost count of her lovers. He suspected that Bill Wells, the golf pro, was the new one. He could always tell when Cilla was making a play for some man—she hadn't even the decency to try to hide the facts from him. These last few years, since she'd been drinking more heavily, she had become increasingly indiscreet. He must talk to her about it—yet he feared the bitter lash of her tongue. She despised him and took no trouble to hide that, either.

They should have been divorced. Gerald knew it as surely as he knew he never could divorce her. Apart from their other troubles which he could not bring himself to think about, there was his position as M.P. always to be weighed in the balance against freedom. Divorce, however commonplace these days, was never a matter for congratulations. The electors preferred happily married, family men with no skeletons in the cupboard. So did the Party. No, he and Cilla were irrevocably tied together and he had to make the best of it.

'I'd like a word with you, Cilla!' he said over the top of his *Times,* behind which he had been hiding.

Cilla Newman glanced up at her husband with her customary expression of boredom. Only her eyes, of such a dark brown as to be almost black, glittered, alive, restless in her thin, sallow face. She did not trouble to make up for her husband and the ravages of twenty years dissolute living showed all too clearly to anyone who cared to study her. Those who saw her 'public' face, would have had difficulty in recognising her now. She wore a blue candlewick dressing gown and feathered mules; her greying hair, dyed a bright blonde, was tied up in a chiffon turban.

'Well, what's wrong now?' she asked. Her eyes took a quick downward glance at the pile of letters by Gerald's plate. He had not yet opened them so he wasn't about to complain about the bills she had run up. There was one particularly large account due in from a London dress shop which she knew would cause a row. She didn't really care. There was nothing much Gerald could do about her bills—other than pay them, she thought scornfully.

She looked at her husband's bald head with loathing. His face, florid and puffy, was far too fat. He should diet but he wouldn't. He was what Cilla understood to be a compulsive eater—turning to food whenever he was upset. These last few years, since he was living on his nerves, he was seldom not eating. He'd put on at least two stones and what few good looks he had once had were lost now beneath a mound of excess fat. His pale blue eyes were set in heavy pouches and he looked a good deal older than his forty-five years.

'Are you going to the club house this morning?' Gerald asked, his mouth twitching in the way it always did when he was introducing a controversial subject with Cilla. He hated himself for this uncontrollable weakness with her. In public, he could talk freely, firmly and convincingly and without the trace of a stammer. In fact, it was his ability to make such good speeches and put them across so well that had got him elected. His maiden speech in the House had been masterly but now, face to face with his wife, he could only stutter. He felt a movement of acute hatred for her because he knew he must and always would be afraid of her.

'Playing golf? Of course I am!' she answered him coldly. 'What in God's name else do you think I've got to do with myself? Ashwyck is hardly a hive of entertainment on a Saturday morning. Or perhaps you'd prefer I joined in on some of those idiotic coffee mornings the Vicar's wife goes in for?'

'Don't be silly, Cilla!' He broke off, his face scarlet as she laughed at his sibilants. 'I just wanted to s-say that I think you s-s-should keep away from Wells . . .'

'Keep away from *Bill*? Are you mad?' Cilla broke in furiously. 'For one thing, I've got a lesson with him at eleven-thirty. You're not really suggesting that when we get back to the club house after my lesson, I say: "Sorry, Bill, but Gerald doesn't want me to have a drink with you so I'll sit at this end of the bar while you go and sit at the other"?'

Gerald slammed down *The Times,* upsetting the pot of marmalade.

'You know perfectly well what I m-m-mean!' he spluttered.

'Jealous, darling?' Cilla asked, her voice suddenly sweet. 'I suppose it is understandable—he does have the most beautiful eyelashes I ever saw on any man, not to mention that Adonis physique. *Must* you have another piece of toast, Gerald? You know you'll end up with a coronary if you put on much more fat.'

Gerald stood up, his heavy bulk towering over the table, his face dark with anger.

'I won't have my wife making a f-fool of

24

herself in public!' he shouted. 'What you do in private I neither know nor care, but you know d-damn well what Ashwyck is like. It'll be all over the place in no time that you're making a play for Wells. If you start an affair with him, I'm t-telling you, Cilla, I'll . . .'

'Yes, Gerald?'

He stared down at her speechless. As usual, she had got the better of him. There wasn't a damn thing he could do to stop her and they both knew it.

'If I'm not re-elected, Cilla, you'll be the one to suffer. You're the one who enjoys the p-prestige of being Milady in this godforsaken village. There was a time when I was ambitious, too, but I'm no longer so sure I care. Don't make your price too high, Cilla, understand? I just m-might resign.'

Her silence accompanied him to the door through which he made an unusually dignified retreat. His heart was pounding with excitement. He knew by his wife's silence, that he had scored a point at last. Cilla had one big weakness—she was a snob, a class snob. At one time she'd been nothing but a sales girl in a suburban drapery store. Her good looks and sharp, amusing personality had helped her to step above her humble beginnings and marriage to Gerald had put her into an entirely different class. She had worked tirelessly to help him forward his political career. He had fondly imagined in those first years that it was for his sake—but he'd soon found out that it was entirely for herself. When they moved to Ashwyck, she, as the M.P.'s wife, had access to all doors that might otherwise have remained closed. The Newmans were invited everywhere.

Gerald himself was of middle-class background. He and his brother Frank had both been educated at a minor public school. Frank had gone in for journalism but Gerald, though younger, was academically the brainier and had gone on to university to study politics and economics. Frank had risen fairly quickly but as far as he was likely to go—to become editor of the local weekly newspaper. But though it had taken Gerald longer to make a name for himself, he'd ended up in a far more influential position than his elder brother. Frank's influence was purely local; Gerald, so he liked to think, could affect the nation! Nevertheless, Frank still treated him like a kid brother. Character-wise, he was by far the stronger of the two. Gerald was, and always had been, weak. He was hopelessly self-indulgent and but for Cilla's persistent ambitions for him, might never have made the necessary effort and sacrifices to reach his present position. He not only ate too much; he drank too much and was bordering on becoming an alcoholic when a car accident some years ago had shaken him so deeply that he knocked off

26

alcohol entirely for a while. Now he tried, not very successfully, to keep his liquid consumption down to a reasonable level.

There was nothing altruistic about Gerald's desire to be a politician. It was merely a way of life, a job which interested him. He had no deep-rooted ancestral associations with Ashwyck, although he and Frank, sons of a doctor, had lived in a neighbouring village as children. He hadn't the slightest desire to better the lot of his constituents. When he took up a cause on their behalf, it was purely a matter of policy to do so and not because he really cared what became of any of the thousands of his supporters. Childless himself, he thought little about the coming generation or its needs and had taken only the smallest necessary interest in the big new Comprehensive school just recently completed. He'd attended the official opening, made a rousing speech on the great benefits the new school would provide and forgotten all about it until he was asked to present prizes on Sport's Day. Whether the school system worked efficiently or otherwise, he neither knew nor cared and was content to be briefed from time to time by the local county councillor who was conveniently of the same political persuasion as himself.

He would have liked a child, Gerald thought, as he made his way to his study. But in the early years there hadn't been the time and later, it was too late. The marriage as such only lasted a few years and had disintegrated with the first of Cilla's affairs. Now, considering his wife coldly, without respect or love, he knew that she could never be a mother. There wasn't a spark of the maternal in her. She was totally selfish.

He shut the study door and began to leaf through the morning mail. But his thoughts were not concentrated on the correspondence. He was thinking about Wells, the young Australian. If Cilla was not willing to be discreet about her interest in him, he hoped very much that Wells would have other ideas. He, Gerald, could get him sacked and Wells must know that. He almost felt sorry for the fellow. He wouldn't find it easy keeping Cilla at arm's length and she could be extremely nasty when rejected. It would take a considerably more sophisticated man than the Australian to handle Cilla with the requisite tact if she'd really made up her mind to have him. If the outcome didn't have possible reflections upon himself, Gerald could almost sit back and enjoy the battle he foresaw.

If he were not much mistaken, Wells had his eye on that pretty little girl, Sally—or was it Sandie?—White. He couldn't place her background but he'd seen her mainly because Cilla spoke so viciously about the girl; criticising either her clothes or her makeup or her behaviour. Not that he, Gerald, could see anything wrong with the girl. He suspected

28

Cilla was jealous because she was young and obviously attractive to the men. Rudgely, that young reporter, was always hanging around and Bill Wells had already dated her once or twice. Cilla wasn't going to find it quite so easy competing with a girl like that, Gerald told himself with satisfaction.

But Sandie was not at the Golf Club this Saturday morning to offer any unconscious resistance to Cilla's campaign to attract Bill. She was doing her best to comfort poor little Julia Forbes in the sitting-room of her flat. The child had obviously been crying all night. This morning her parents had tried to force her to tell them what was wrong but she'd been too afraid to confess the truth and had allowed them to think it was nothing more than a quarrel with Tony Dodd that had upset her.

'Oh, Miss White,' the girl sobbed, 'if you could have seen my Dad's face. He looked straight at me and said: "You're not in any trouble with this boy, are you?" and I nearly died. I thought he'd found out somehow—but he was just guessing. I think if he knew he'd half kill me. I daren't tell him, I daren't! And if I did he might not believe it was Mike Shaw and blame Tony.'

Sandy looked at Rudge over the girl's head. When Julia called at the flat he had been on the point of leaving, but she had burst into tears immediately upon entering the room so, inadvertently, he had become involved in the situation.

'I suppose Julia's parents will have to be told?' Sandie asked him. But even before he spoke, she knew what his answer would be.

'Julia is only fifteen. But you've nothing to be afraid of, Julia,' he added, putting a hand comfortingly on the girl's shoulder. 'Of course it will be a shock to your parents but they won't hurt you. It wasn't your fault!'

Julia looked up at him with brimming eyes.

'*You* believe that, but will *they*? They might think I . . . I . . .'

'Nonsense, Julia!' Sandie broke in sharply. 'They know as well as I do that you aren't promiscuous. I'll come with you if you like. We'll tell them together.'

'Oh, Miss White, will you?' The child's pale face shone with relief. 'I wouldn't be so frightened if you were there. But . . . my Dad will never get over it. Oh, what am I going to do!'

'Before anything else, we'll pay a visit to the school doctor,' Sandie said practically. 'Let's make quite sure first of all that your fears are justified, Julia. They may not be. Then we must have a talk with the headmistress. If Mrs Sinclair agrees, I'll come with you to tell your parents.'

When Julia finally left, still pale but a little more composed now she knew Sandie intended to stand beside her, Rudge's optimistic cheerfulness gave way to a frown.

'You realise we ought to be reporting this to the police? If rape it was, it is a serious offence and you and I are concealing evidence!'

Sandie grimaced.

'Oh, darling, don't say things like that. Think what a case such as this would do to a sensitive child like Julia on top of all the rest she's going to go through. Imagine that wretched child having to go through all the sordid details in public. No, Rudge, I won't do my civic duty, if that's what you're asking of me, not if it means the child has to suffer any more than she is already.'

'We may not be able to prevent it,' Rudge said thoughtfully. 'I know it's awful but so is rape. What that boy did to Julia, he could do to another child.'

'Well, *you're* not supposed to know anything about it,' Sandie said pointedly. 'And as far as I am concerned, nothing is a fact yet. It could all be a figment of Julia's imagination. I'm not supposed to report *that* to the police, I presume?'

Rudge grinned.

'Well, that's a matter for you to decide, my love. In fact, my advice to you is to keep out of it as much as you can. Let the headmistress or the doctor or Julia's parents do the necessary. She may be your pupil but she isn't your responsibility and I'm not having you dragged into anything if I can help it.'

He saw her raised eyebrows and again he grinned.

'Well, I know I don't have much of a say yet in your life, my girl, but as your fiancé, I soon will have and I intend to look after you whether you like it or not. Understand?'

'The big he-man, eh?' Sandie teased, but allowed him to take her in his arms. 'I think I shall rather enjoy being looked after,' she added between his kisses.

Sandie had been orphaned early in her life and had been brought up by elderly grandparents, both of whom died when she was still in her teens. She had looked after herself since then, living in digs during her three years at art college and fending for herself.

Teaching had seemed the obvious career for her, providing her with the security she felt necessary and which would not have been there if she had gone in for commercial art which at one time she had contemplated. Now, after eighteen months in a school, she knew that she had made the right choice. She enjoyed her contact with the pupils and had a natural relationship with them without foregoing any of the necessary authority they needed. She had started on her arrival at Ashwyck by living in digs but when a row of new shops had been built down by the station with little modern flats over them, at not unreasonable rents, Sandie had decided to make a home for herself. She could afford the rent and had enough saved from her salary to furnish the flat to her taste.

Moving in had been fun and she had been perfectly content, going out occasionally with Bill Wells and with Max Hampshire, one of the few unmarried masters at the school. It wasn't until Rudge had arrived in Ashwyck six months ago that life had begun to take on a new dimension. Now her free time became considerably more important. The holiday breaks at Christmas and Easter had been far too short for all the things she and Rudge wanted to do together. Without knowing it, he had begun to play an important part in her life, not just as escort but as friend, confidant, adviser. She had become dependent upon him and couldn't contemplate a life now in which Rudge was not somewhere around.

'Love me a little?' he asked, ruffling her hair.

'Rather too much, I think!' Sandie replied breathlessly. 'Time we went out to lunch, darling. If we stay here, I might. . .'

'Let's stay here!' Rudge broke in grinning, but Sandie moved quickly out of the circle of his arms.

'No! Out!' she said firmly. 'Had you forgotten you were taking me down to Baker's Pool to visit "The scene of the crime"?'

'Too right, I had forgotten!' Rudge said, his

face suddenly serious. 'Shows how bad you are for me, Sandie—your charms have even put the sleuth reporter off the scent of the crime. Put some thick shoes on, darling. It'll probably be muddy down there after last night's rain. If we get a move on, we can still go before lunch.'

Sandie went into the tiny bedroom and searched for some heavy golf shoes. The door was open and she called through to Rudge:

'Can't think what you're hoping to *see* there!'

'Nothing, I suppose!' Rudge called back. 'But I've made up my mind to do a really good article on my Mystery Man and I want to get the atmosphere right.'

Ten minutes later they stood side by side on the edge of Baker's Pool. The sun had gone in and with the overhanging trees and heavy undergrowth, there was a dark green gloom around them, reflected in the thick swirling waters below. Sandie shivered.

'Grim sort of place,' she murmured.

Rudge nodded.

'The water looks pretty deep, too!' he said, throwing in a lump of rotten wood and watching it twisted this way and that by a strong but hidden current.

Water poured down into the pool from a culvert running under the main road fifteen feet above their heads. From the road, unless one stopped to look over the stone wall, the pool itself would be invisible. It was about a mile out of Ashwyck village and there was nothing on either side of the road but fields and woods. It was isolated, with no noise to disturb the wild life with the exception of an occasional passing car.

'Not a bad spot for a murder,' Sandie remarked with an attempt at a flippancy she was not really feeling.

'I *must* find those records!' Rudge said thoughtfully as he helped her up the steep bank, slippery with sodden grass and mud. 'I want to know exactly where the chap fell in and what he was doing when he fell, *if* he fell and wasn't pushed!'

'Fishing?' Sandie suggested as they reached road level and stopped to wipe the mud on tufts of grass by the car.

'Could be. Yet that sexton didn't describe him as a fisherman. One wonders if there was tackle lying around. It's funny about those files, Sandie. Why should those particular weeks be missing?'

They climbed into the car and Rudge switched on the engine. He glanced at Sandie's face and saw she was smiling.

'You'll make a story of it even if there isn't one,' she teased him.

Rudge slid into gear. He backed the car and turned round towards Ashwyck. There was no smile on his face as he said:

'If files have been tampered with or records

are missing, there's always a story behind it! And I'm going to unearth it if it's the last thing I do.'

Sandie shivered despite the warmth of the car's interior. She glanced at the man beside her and felt a sudden rush of love for him.

'Be careful, Rudge!' she said.

It was only later she wondered what had made her choose those words for as yet, there was no reason to suppose Rudge or anyone else in Ashwyck, including herself, was in danger.

THREE

Rudge looked across the desk at his editor with mounting annoyance tinged with surprise.

'I accept that you have the final say-so as to what is printed in the *Stanfield Observer*,' he said, making an effort to talk calmly and logically. The argument had been fierce and heated until the moment when Frank Newman announced flatly that he did not intend to publish an article on the Mystery Man no matter what Rudge unearthed about him. 'All I'm asking—and surely you appreciate I've the right to ask—is what you have against the idea?'

Frank Newman met the young man's flushed face with a cold glance from narrowed steel-grey eyes. With his thin, aquiline face, the heavy dark brows and pointed nose, he bore little resemblance to his brother, Gerald. Gerald's was a self-indulgent face. Frank's was austere, slightly donnish, though he did possess a wry sense of humour which, when it showed itself, made the man more human and likeable.

On the whole Rudge had got along very well with him, despite the disparity in their ages and outlooks. Rudge was very much a product of the new generation, his hair cut into the neck where Frank's remaining few grey hairs were closely cropped at the back and sides, Rudge wore casual modern clothes and Frank always a dark navy or charcoal suit of conventional style, with shirt and tie.

But despite his rather old-fashioned appearance, Frank Newman was reasonably progressive in outlook and still open-minded enough to accept most of Rudge's new ideas. In fact, until now, they had always managed to discuss and agree on the type of articles Rudge would write and it was seldom Frank altered any of his finished copy.

'Certainly you've the right to ask why I won't go along with this particular idea,' he answered his young reporter coolly. 'But I've the right to reject whatever I don't think topical or suitable for my paper. As I said just now, this is digging up the past. The man, whoever he was, died three years ago. No one knew him and no one at that time could prove whether his death was accidental or otherwise. The police closed the file and the public lost interest—it was a seven day wonder and that's all. I see no point whatever in going back to it. If nothing was found out about him at the time, it certainly couldn't be now. Forget it, Rudgely. I'm not interested.'

Rudge drew a deep breath. He couldn't fully explain why he should feel so het-up about this particular idea. What Newman said made sense—it *was* delving backwards and everyone knew a good newspaper looked forward. All the same, he had a hunch about this story—an instinct he couldn't have explained but which kept nagging at him that he was 'on to something'. He believed in playing these hunches. In the past, they had paid off.

'Look, Mr Newman,' he said slowly, curbing his own impatience and trying to keep calm, 'I appreciate your right to turn the idea down. I also appreciate that in the past you've very seldom balked when I've been dead keen to do something. But you may change your mind when you hear a piece of news I should perhaps have given you before we started to discuss the whole business—namely that the *Observer* files are incomplete. There is nothing at all in any of the remaining back copies of the *Observer* about the case. It's my belief someone has deliberately removed the relevant ones. Why? And who?'

Rudge was not in the least surprised to see that he now had his editor's attention. Newman was staring at him with an entirely new expression on his face.

'When did you find this out?' he asked abruptly.

'Friday evening. I'm absolutely sure about it, Mr Newman—there isn't a single copy referring to the Mystery Man. It stands to reason the *Observer* would have reported the case, however briefly. Yet there isn't even a paragraph on the inquest. You must admit it's odd to say the least of it. All the other years are complete—only that part of the year is missing.'

The older man turned away sharply and walked over to the window. He stood for a moment with his back to Rudge, staring down into the busy High Street. When he spoke he sounded suddenly old, tired.

'I expect there's a perfectly logical explanation, Rudgely. Perhaps the police wanted to look through them and didn't return them or some half-witted sub replaced them under the wrong year. Take my advice and don't waste any more time on this—in fact, that's an order, Rudgely. There's more than enough for you to do on this paper without looking for work. I want you to cover the parent/teacher meeting at the school this afternoon and this morning I want you to interview that R.A.F. chap who won the V.C. in the last war. He's just published a book which is causing quite a stir.'

He paused and turned round to meet Rudge's disappointed face. 'Sorry, Rudgely, but my mind's made up. When you step into my shoes, which you well might in a year or two when I retire, you'll be Editor and you can make the decisions. Meanwhile, I do and I have to tell you to forget your Mystery Man. No doubt he was just a tramp who fell into the pool—or a drunk. I doubt there's a story to tell. Off you go now, and see what you can dig up from the war ace.'

Rudge left the office with mixed feelings. He could see Newman's point of view—the story was old hat. Time was pressing and he had plenty to do without making work for himself. On the other hand, he couldn't entirely rid himself of that hunch. He knew he wouldn't be at peace with himself until he could work it out of his system. Newman had ordered him to pack it in but what he, Rudge, did in his own free time was his own affair. When he'd finished work there was nothing to stop him paying a visit to the local police station, making a few enquiries there. The *Observer*'s records might be missing but the police would certainly not have 'mislaid' theirs! Perhaps if he could unearth just a few facts he could do a sample article and show it to Newman, raise the old boy's interest in spite of himself.

In a happier frame of mind now that he had decided to follow up the story for himself rather than for his paper, Rudge got into his old blue Ford and set off in the direction of the cottage where the elderly ex-Battle-of-Britain pilot had lived an uneventful life since his retirement. On the way there, he had to drive past the Comprehensive. He thought of Sandie and wondered how she was coping this morning. In the lunch break she was accompanying poor little Julia to the headmistress.

Naturally kind hearted and always soft where children were concerned, Rudge felt a deep compassion for the child. Maybe it was not too late for her to have an abortion but that kind of business could ruin her whole life. It seemed terrible to him that at the tender age of fifteen, a child's emotional future should already be in jeopardy through no fault of her own. Apart from his own view of the girl—she'd seemed a quiet, serious little thing—he was prepared to take Sandie's word for it that Julia hadn't in any way brought this on herself. Sandie, for all her comparative inexperience, was remarkably perspicacious for a twenty-one year old. There were even times when he found himself asking her advice; depending upon her opinions and approval. But that, he told himself with a grin, was Love. Now that he knew he wanted to marry her, their relationship had subtly changed. His happiness depended upon her and he had no intention of letting it slip through his fingers now that it was within reach. He would marry Sandie just as soon as she agreed to marry him. And meanwhile, he'd give her as little time as possible to better her acquaintance with Bill Wells. There was to be no competition for her affections from the Australian if he could help it.

Rudge did not often think about it now, but a few years ago he'd been engaged to a girl with whom he'd been deeply in love. Literally at the eleventh hour—a week before their wedding—she'd thrown him over and gone off with an American she'd only met a few weeks earlier. It had been a terrible shock to Rudge. His parents, elderly but devoted, had tried their hardest to make him see that he was well rid of her but he'd gone pretty well to pieces nevertheless. It was on this account he had thrown over his job on a Midlands paper and decided to make a completely fresh start in the South. He'd seen the vacancy on the *Stanfield Observer* and although Ashwyck was only a pinpoint on the map and he'd known nothing at all of Sussex, he'd written for an interview and landed the job.

The new environment, new faces, new paper, all helped him to look back on his broken engagement in a calmer, more resigned frame of mind. Gradually he'd found he had stopped thinking about the girl and his thoughts were taken up instead with a new girl—Sandie White. At first he'd looked on her as an escape from his unhappy memories of the past. But gradually, without him realising at what stage it had happened, he found Sandie was necessary to him—for herself. It was not only that he found her physically attractive, but he enjoyed every moment in her company. Frequently they argued passionately but on controversial issues outside themselves; whether America had the right attitude to Russia; whether Comprehensive schools really did offer more than the old Grammar schools. On the main topics of life they seemed to be in surprising agreement. They both wanted a large family, being only children themselves; they both preferred country to town life; they both felt that money should never be the first consideration; that principles were only worth anything if one was prepared to back them to the hilt. In all their discussions, they agreed where it was important to agree.

There was only one snag to falling in love with Sandie. Marriage now must mean settling down. Rudge tried to push the idea to the back of his mind but at moments of truthful self-analysis, he had to admit that he didn't really want to tie himself to remaining in Ashwyck.

Sandie had the kind of job she wanted at

the school; a nice little flat. She liked the quiet country life and wanted to remain here. In a way, he agreed that it wasn't a bad kind of life or a bad place to live. It was his job on the *Stanfield Observer* he was not too sure about. At one time in his life, he'd had strong ideas about becoming a crime reporter or at least, a top reporter on a National paper. To have to resign himself at the age of twenty-seven to a very third-rate job on the *Observer* was more than he felt able to stomach. If he decided one day he wanted to move to something bigger and better, it would mean uprooting Sandie. He wasn't sure yet whether she was prepared to do this. She was very independent. She was also very modern in her outlook. Marriage with a girl like Sandie would mean a partnership of equals. She wasn't the type to believe that her husband's career was all that mattered. She wanted— and had a right to—a career of her own.

Of course, Rudge told himself, Sandie could move schools. There were plenty of Comprehensives in London. But Sandie did not like London life. She had once told him she would never go back to live in a big city.

Rudge sighed. Life was never quite so simple as it often seemed at first glance. The question of where they lived would have to be brought up for discussion soon. No problem, Rudge reminded himself grimly, was solved by hiding it or pretending it didn't exist. But there seemed little point in raising it at the moment when his mind was not clear as to his own future. He knew the chances of his becoming editor in Frank Newman's place were reasonably good, though it would be several years at least before the old boy retired. But it was a chance, not a certainty. If the hitherto good relationship between them deteriorated for any reason, he, Rudge, could just as easily find himself out on his ear, jobless. Not that this was likely. Until this morning he'd been pretty much of one mind with his editor. Still, this morning had shown him that even the best of working partnerships can go wrong. He didn't much care for the idea of *having* to agree with Newman regardless of his own opinions. He'd always been a free agent until now. The prospect of being anything else held no appeal and he knew he would have to take this question up with Sandie. Before marriage. If it came to the point at any time in the future, she must be prepared to back him to the hilt; move away from Ashwyck no matter how much she herself wanted to remain in her present job.

Suddenly, Rudge's mood lightened. Marriage inevitably meant kids. When they came along, Sandie would have to give up her job, anyway for a while. When this happened, he'd be as free as he was now to up roots and get a job elsewhere. He might do well to start saving some money for a change. There could come a time when he'd need something behind him to tide him over between jobs. With a wife and children, he couldn't go on living from day to day the way he had in the past.

Responsibilities! Rudge told himself with a grin. He could hardly believe he was voluntarily saddling himself with the very thing he'd always sought to avoid. He'd once fondly imagined himself the confirmed bachelor. But he'd been caught just like all the other mugs and unlike the last girl, this time he was in love for keeps. Or so he very much hoped. If a break came, it would be of Sandie's making, not his. He really loved her; really wanted her. He was honest enough to admit that to a large extent it was a physical attraction. But there was lots more to it than a mere desire to put her to bed and keep her there! He respected her opinion; enjoyed her conversation, her company. And it mattered to him that she felt the same way about him.

It was only at this stage in his reflections that Rudge realised he didn't *really* know her very well at all. They had drifted from companionship to love so casually that there had never arisen a necessity for probing very deeply beneath the surface. He knew only what she *seemed* to be. Now he wanted to know what kind of woman she really was; her deepest thoughts; her subconscious desires;

her dreams; her aversions.

He had arrived without knowing it at his destination. With that peculiar knack he had always had, he was able to sweep his mind free from personal thoughts. He could always be totally single-minded about his work. That was what made him such a good reporter. Love and its subsidiaries must wait until the completion of the job in hand.

FOUR

Cilla Newman bent and picked her ball off the putting green, then shouldered her golf bag. She turned and looked at the man beside her speculatively.

'End of lesson. I've had enough for this morning. Bill,' she said casually. 'Let's go back to the Club House and have a drink.'

Bill Wells shrugged his shoulders.

'Okay, Mrs Newman, if you're tired . . .'

'Cilla!' she corrected him, frowning.

'Cilla!' he echoed, but he avoided meeting her eyes. He knew very well that she found him attractive—he wasn't born yesterday— but he did not intend to become involved. He knew from past experience the folly of playing around with married women—especially middle-aged women and even more especially unhappily married middle-aged woman. One could never be sure they would keep an affair casual, or private. Cilla Newman wasn't exactly the reticent type. From what he knew of her, she took little trouble to hide her feelings about anyone and she certainly hadn't troubled to conceal her interest in him.

Together they walked back across the golf course towards the Club House. It was a beautiful morning, sunny and bright without being too warm . . . an English Spring day living up to its reputation.

Reputation! Bill thought wryly as he waited for Cilla to precede him over the wooden bridge across the stream. In that one word lay the reason why he wouldn't play ball with Cilla Newman. She was by no means unattractive and he was minus a girl friend at the moment, but he dared not become involved. If she were more discreet . . . but he sensed rather than knew that this word was foreign to her make-up. He didn't want to lose his job here as golf pro. He was well paid—had a decent little bungalow on the perimeter of the course—and had settled down fairly happily in Ashwyck. Occasionally he toyed with the idea of returning to Australia, but he was in no hurry. He had no ties over there and he liked England. He got on well with most of the club members and with the women in particular.

Bill knew that he was attractive to the opposite sex. Tall, broad shouldered, athletic and in superb condition, he could measure up pretty well to any of the other unattached males around the place. Not that there were all that many bachelors in Ashwyck. Most of the men who frequented the Golf Club were married, with odd exceptions like Rudgely, the young reporter, and one or two grown-up sons of married couples who commuted with their fathers to London and played golf at the weekends.

Childless women like Cilla Newman, Bill reflected, were always the worst. He suspected it had something to do with a subconscious realisation that they'd missed out somehow, in being complete women. A woman, he felt, needed to be a mother at some stage of her life. There was no doubting the fact that this one was frustrated; but he realised this was probably due to an unhappy marriage. Everyone could see that she was bored to tears with Newman. He, himself, found Gerald a dreadful old bore and the fellow hadn't weathered the years well the way his wife had. For a woman in her forties, Cilla Newman was surprisingly attractive in a hard, brittle way. She wasn't really his type yet he was man enough to be flattered by her obvious interest in him; and conceited enough to be amused by the blatant way in which she was trying to entice him into an affair.

It was a pity, Bill reflected, as they neared the Club House, that she was quite such a prominent member of local society.

Everything Cilla did would be talked about and he didn't want trouble.

Nevertheless, he wasn't going to be entirely unresponsive to her advances. He was feeling not a little put out by his failure to make headway with young Sandra. He'd fallen more than a little in love with that girl. For a little while, it had looked as if she might have some time for him, too—until Rudgely arrived on the scene and somehow managed to muscle in. Now Sandra was seldom out of his company and he, Bill, seldom saw her alone except for her golf lessons. His nose was sadly out of joint and he found a certain consolation in Cilla's attentions. If nothing else, they soothed his ego.

As they walked past the rows of parked cars, Cilla said suddenly:

'Must we have drinks with that same dreary old crowd? Why don't we pop off in my car to the Waterman's Arms for a change?'

Bill hesitated.

'I'm on duty . . . Cilla!' he added. He never used her Christian name in public despite her continual reminders to him that she disliked being addressed as Mrs Newman. She gave him a long searching look.

'So what? There's still half an hour of my lesson to go. If I choose to have it in the Waterman's Arms, who's to object?'

Bill was tempted but he shook his head none the less.

'Sorry, Cilla, I'd love to—but I can't. I have to see a chappie in my shop just before lunch—he wants some new clubs. I'd never get down to the village and back by twelve-thirty. Some other time.'

His refusal exasperated her. She had sensed his hesitation and known she had been on the verge of success. He'd thought better of it and she wanted to know why. Was he afraid of Gerald? Or of village gossip? Of *her*? Or was he just 'not interested'? She couldn't be sure.

'Some other time, then!' she said coolly and was further annoyed by the grin that spread over his face. He could afford to smile. For a moment, he held the cards and she had to follow suit. But that would change. She wasn't used to being rejected and once Bill was under her thumb she would make him pay for these weeks of playing hard to get. For all he might like to project an image of being God's gift to women, she was pretty sure he was fairly uncomplicated. His sophistication was very much a veneer, covering a brash immaturity. He was the kind of man, unintellectual, physical, whom she could dominate easily enough when it came to sex.

As she followed his tall, muscular figure into the bar, she felt a moment of sheer physical weakness. She wanted this man. She didn't care how long it took or what methods she had to use, she intended to have him sooner or later. Ever since the New Year's

Eve dance when she had felt what it was like to be in his arms, she had thought of little else. It had ruined her relationship with Philip Hurst, who, until then, had provided ample compensation for the sterility of her life with Gerald. Now Philip was no longer desirable to her.

Whilst waiting for her brandy, Cilla thought about the man who had been her lover for more years than she cared to remember. She both disliked and feared him yet he had held a certain fascination for her. At one time, Philip Hurst had been a source of endless interest to the Ashwyck inhabitants. An artist, and as far as anyone knew, unknown and unmarried, Philip lived alone in a tiny cottage two miles beyond Baker's Pool, in the depths of Stanfield Woods. There was no road to the cottage, at one time used by a gamekeeper; only a rough track, boggy in winter and barely useable even in summer except by occasional hikers.

Philip himself, a man of nearly fifty, lived like a hermit, never appearing in the local pubs and only visiting the village on brief excursions to renew his supplies. There were no electricity or mains services at the cottage. No one ever went there and as far as anyone knew, there were never any visitors. Philip had all the outward appearances of an eccentric, too. His fair, greying hair was nearly always shoulder length. He usually wore a heavy paint-stained polo-necked jersey and equally dirty grey flannel trousers. As he was tall and gauntly thin, coming upon him suddenly in the woods, he could easily be mistaken for a dark spectre and the village kids kept their distance.

Cilla had first heard of him from the Vicar. Her interest had initially been aroused when she learned that Philip had practically flung the Vicar off the premises.

'A Godless man!' the Vicar described him, shocked and indignant that his efforts to be sociable had failed so dismally. Amused, Cilla had decided to go and see for herself.

Her visit, of necessity on foot, had been one of the most interesting Cilla had ever spent in Ashwyck. It turned out to be the first of many. It was some months, however, before she was able to sort out the facts from her strange first impressions of the eccentric artist. One of the truths which had emerged was that Philip Hurst couldn't really paint. Although his cottage was piled ceiling high in every room with canvasses, there wasn't one picture worth more than the price of the canvas it was painted on. Little as Cilla herself knew about art, even she could see that in all of them, some essential was missing. It explained why he would never, never discuss his work. All he ever said about it was a simple:

'It's what I like doing!'

She suspected that he made himself believe—perhaps really did believe—that one day he would paint something worthwhile. But his strange, silent bitter conversation indicated to her that he had long since lost hope. He was rude, critical, cynical and evil. He'd been so from the first. But it hadn't stopped her permitting him silently and efficiently making love to her that very first afternoon when, seeing her standing in the open doorway watching him, he had told her either to get out or lie down. Amused, intrigued—most of all bored—she'd chosen to do the latter and been surprised to find herself caught up in a passion that far outweighed her own violent appetites and through which he dominated her completely.

A little afraid, she'd returned home resolved not to go back. But of course, she *had* returned just as he had known she would. From then on, she visited him regularly, though never by arrangement or appointment. He was never a lover in the true sense of the word. He simply possessed her. Remembering the Vicar's description of him as 'A Godless man', Cilla sometimes told herself wryly that she was 'possessed by the devil'! At first she felt, rather than knew, that he was evil. He seemed to have cut himself off deliberately because he despised all humanity. He never spoke of people except in the most derogatory terms. Once or twice, Cilla had tried to probe into his past but he told her fiercely to mind her own business. She wondered about him;

whether he had been a criminal; had done time; whether he could have been cast out by society or had cast himself out, as he stated. He was obviously an educated man from the upper middle classes, but she never learned any details of his background.

It wasn't until a year after she had first met him she discovered her instincts were sound and that this strange man really was as the Vicar described him—Godless. He had it in his power to ruin two people who had never done him a moment's harm. Coldly, ruthlessly, he blackmailed them, knowing that they *would* pay for his silence and extorting from them not enough to ruin them but sufficient to be able to amass over the years a comfortable wad of capital for himself. He was far too clever to ask too much of the goose that was laying his golden eggs.

'I'm having nothing more to do with you, Philip,' Cilla had told him when she discovered what he was doing. 'Heaven knows I'm not a very moral person but I draw the line at this.'

Philip had laughed in her face.

'My dear Cilla,' he said coldly, 'don't forget your reputation is at stake. I shouldn't hesitate to expose you as my mistress. Of course you'll go on seeing me.'

She'd realised then that she'd been a fool ever to become involved with him, but equally, she saw that it was a waste of time and energy trying to fight a man like Philip Hurst. If the price of his silence was the continuation of her weekly visits to him, the simplest way was to continue them. Though she might hate and fear him, it did not alter the strange physical satisfaction he gave her. After all, she told herself, she never had *liked* him; nor he her. But with Bill Wells it was different. The affair with Philip had lost its novelty. Moreover, he was a man of fifty. Bill was in his prime and she was madly attracted by him.

She looked over her drink at him and said softly:

'You must come and have dinner with us one evening, Bill. You haven't been to our house yet, have you? Why not come one day this week: Thursday? Or Wednesday? I'm pretty sure Gerald will be home both nights.'

Bill returned her glance. He was both annoyed and amused. She had put him on a spot. He could hardly find at an instant's notice an excuse for two consecutive nights of the week.

'That's very kind of you. May I let you know?'

'Of course! I'll be along tomorrow morning for my lesson. You can tell me then,' she replied. She put a hand lightly on Bill's arm, feeling the muscles stiffen momentarily beneath her touch. 'I've some rather nice new tapes,' she went on smoothly. 'Or would you prefer I get a fourth and we played some bridge?'

'I enjoy a game of bridge,' Bill said non-committally. He watched the sudden frown crease Cilla's forehead and knew he had annoyed her. He didn't really care. Better to be safe than sorry. Besides, he had just seen Sandra White come into the Club House and he wanted to be rid of Cilla Newman so he could go and talk to the girl. For once she wasn't with Rudgely.

Fortunately for him, Cilla stalked off in a huff, hoping to indicate to him that she was displeased with his evasiveness. Bill grinned to himself and forgetting her, went over to Sandra.

'Come and have a drink,' he said, thinking how pretty she looked with that bright hair and her cheeks a soft warm red. 'You look as if you could do with one.'

Sandie forced a smile.

'To tell the truth, I've just had a blazing row with Rudge . . . with Bob Rudgely!' she said unguardedly. She was so cross with Rudge she hadn't quite got herself under control. Now, as Bill tucked an arm in hers and helped her on to a bar stool, she half regretted her remark.

'What's that chappie been up to?' Bill asked. 'Want his neck wrung for him, Sandra?'

Suddenly she laughed.

'No, of course not! It's not as bad as all

that. As a matter of fact, I expect I'm the one who is being unreasonable. Forget it.'

Bill ordered drinks and turned back to the girl beside him.

'I don't want to forget it!' he said. 'It's a Big Day with a capital B if you've chucked him over. You know I've just been waiting for a moment like this to . . .'

'Bill, please!' Sandra broke in, embarrassed. 'I didn't mean we'd had a *serious* row. It's really very silly. I was annoyed because he cut our lunch date, that's all. My first afternoon class isn't until three on a Wednesday so we have a standing arrangement to . . .' She broke off, regretting that she had revealed her personal feelings to her companion. 'There's nothing more to it than a bit of childish pique on my side.'

'His loss, my gain,' Bill said quickly. 'Lunch with me!'

On the point of refusing, Sandra hesitated. Why not? She'd been going to lunch here alone. Bill was good company and it served Rudge right. If he'd had a reasonable excuse she wouldn't have been so annoyed with him, but to cut lunch because he couldn't wait to go and look at a lot of mouldy old files . . .

She sighed, forgetting for the moment the man beside her. Rudge was becoming obsessed with this Mystery Man story. And it wasn't even as if his editor wanted the story. When Rudge had called at the school to cancel their lunch appointment, he'd spared enough time to tell her about his interview with Frank Newman but couldn't, apparently, spare the time to listen to her account of what had been happening to poor little Julia.

On reflection, Sandra told herself, she was the one who was being unreasonable, not Rudge. He was a reporter and he was, so he fondly imagined, on to a story. She would have to get used to the idea, as his wife, of having him rush off at all times of the day or night. But his enthusiasm had boiled over at the wrong psychological moment. She'd been waiting all morning to tell him that Mrs Sinclair had sent Julia off to the school doctor and it would be a day or more before they knew for a certainty whether the poor child really was pregnant. Most of all, she had wanted to tell Rudge that Mrs Sinclair had decided not to make any move to report the matter to the police or to Julia's parents until the fact was established.

Now, thinking it over with half a glass of shandy inside her, Sandra could see how stupidly she had behaved, rushing off and leaving Rudge in a huff, telling him she might not be able to see him this evening as *she* was busy!

'Where are you going now?' he'd called after her.

'Golf Club—to lunch with Bill!' she'd shouted back. Until then nothing had been further from her thoughts.

Rudge had turned his car and picked her up as she reached the school gates.

'I'll run you up there!' he offered with steely politeness.

'I'll find my own way, thank you!' she had retorted childishly.

But Rudge had called her bluff and landed her here at the Club nonetheless. She'd been forced, if she didn't want to lose face, to walk into the Club House. It had its funny side that Bill should have been here on his own and actually invited her to lunch.

'Funny kid. What are you laughing at all of a sudden?' he said now. 'Share the joke!'

But she wouldn't. It seemed disloyal to Rudge. Instead, she told Bill she was unofficially engaged. Bill's smile faded.

'Are you quite sure, Sandra?' he asked. 'I mean, sure you love him?'

Sandra finished her shandy and put her glass down on the bar.

'Yes! I'm as sure as anyone can be. Aren't you going to congratulate me?'

'No, I'm not!' Bill said flatly. 'It's no cause for celebration when the prettiest girl member of this club gets herself tied up. I take a dim view.'

Sandra laughed.

'I'm not tied up yet, Bill!' she said. 'That is, if you still want to buy me lunch?'

'You bet I do. What's more, I'm going to tell you something, Miss Sandra White. I don't go along with this engagement. I think you're far too good for a chappie like Rudgely. You can tell him I said so and you can tell him I'm going to put as many spokes in his wheel as I can. Frankly, I can't see what you see in him!'

His voice was teasing but with an underlying note of seriousness which did not escape Sandie. In the same casual tone, she said:

'I just happen to love him, Bill. Don't ask me why.'

'Maybe tomorrow you'll come to your senses and realise you don't "just happen to love him" any more!' Bill suggested. 'When that happens, you come straight and tell me, Sandra. I'm what you might call an interested party, see?'

'I'll remember that!' Sandra said with mock seriousness. 'If in doubt, refer to Bill Wells, professional golfer, professional mender of broken hearts. Any other qualifications?'

'Don't be flippant—I'm in earnest,' Bill said, suddenly aware of the fact that he did mean every word he said. He hadn't realised until the moment Sandra told him she was engaged, just how much he'd been thinking about her himself. He hadn't taken her friendship with Bob Rudgely all that seriously . . . imagined it was just a passing flirtation that would wear off. He had had no idea that Sandra was getting serious about the fellow, or that Rudgely would ever contemplate asking her to marry him. Rudgely didn't strike him as the marrying kind. One simply didn't see him as husband and father. But then what bachelor, including himself, seemed the part until the right girl came along and put such thoughts into a chap's head?

'Damn it, Sandra, I'm too late, aren't I?' he said, suddenly deeply depressed.

Sandra, surprised and just a little embarrassed because she knew he wasn't teasing now, said gently:

'I'm afraid so, Bill. I'm sorry!'

He held Sandra's gaze for a long moment.

'Don't forget, will you, that I'm here if ever you want me. Now, let's forget it and have that lunch.'

FIVE

Later that afternoon Rudge was waiting for Sandra at the school gates. He jumped out of his car as he saw her approaching. Taking her acquiescence completely for granted, he bundled her into the passenger seat. He seemed to have forgotten their lunch-time tiff.

'Sandie, I've masses to tell you!' he began excitedly as he put the old Ford into gear and drove off in the direction of Sandie's flat. 'My session at the police station turned out to be far more rewarding than I had dared to hope. Do you know, darling . . .'

He broke off, suddenly sensing something wrong from Sandra's continued silence.

'What's up?' he asked. 'You've very quiet!'

The girl beside him drew a deep sigh of exasperation. It was so difficult to stay annoyed with Rudge yet she could not entirely quell that nagging irritation with him because, newly engaged though they were, he was putting this Mystery Man story of his before her in order of importance. It was obvious he hadn't even given her a thought.

'I've a bit of a headache,' she replied, not altogether untruthfully. 'Too much wine at lunchtime, I expect. I told Bill not to order that second bottle. I can't drink and work in the afternoon.'

Now she did have Rudge's full attention. He turned to look at her and narrowly missed running into the back of a bus drawing in at the kerb and stopping when he wasn't expecting it.

'You mean you did lunch with Bill Wells?' he asked, sounding more surprised than angry.

'Why not? Bill wanted my company.'

Rudge frowned. He didn't like the idea of Sandie spending any time at all with Wells, let alone eating *à deux* with him. Yet he knew he hadn't the right to object when he himself had stood Sandie up.

'Look, darling, I'm sorry about lunch,' he said. 'I thought you understood. I should have explained the situation in more detail. You see, Newman had given me a couple of jobs to do during the morning and afternoons so I knew I couldn't get down to the police station unless I went in my lunch hour.'

'You did explain!' Sandra said, more coolly than she had intended. In fact, she had not meant this situation to develop as it was doing. She had wanted Rudge to be a little jealous of Bill—to know she objected to being put on one side so casually, but that was all. Now, somehow, Rudge was making it worse—making her understand that he expected her to accept the fact that he had more important things to do than escort her around.

'Well, if you aren't annoyed about that, what's wrong?' Rudge asked. 'You aren't being your usual self at all.'

'Perhaps I don't feel what you call "my usual self",' Sandra acknowledged. 'Or perhaps I'm not the kind of girl you've fondly imagined I was . . . the sweet understanding little woman in the background.'

To her surprise, Rudge laughed.

'I don't want a "sweet understanding little woman",' he said as he pulled up in front of the flats and switched off the engine. 'I prefer girls with fire and spirit and initiative.'

'Even if they are demanding and determined and have strong opinions about

64

how a newly acquired fiancé should behave?'

Rudge reached out a hand and gently pulled Sandie's face round so that she was forced to look into his eyes.

'Even then!' he said. Disregarding the passers-by on the street, he kissed her fiercely and possessively.

'So much for Bill!' Sandie thought as she disengaged herself breathlessly from Rudge's arms. There was something about this man which she found hard to define but which attracted her in a way she found almost frightening. At the back of her mind it occurred to her that if she did marry him, life might not always be very easy. Rudge was as strong willed as she knew herself to be. They would probably fight like cat and dog. But at the same time, there was this strange affinity which made her feel she belonged to him. Was it just a physical bond she asked herself, as she preceded Rudge up to her flat? Certainly physical attraction played a large part. She wanted him and knew that he wanted her. But a marriage had to be based on a great deal more than physical attraction if it was to succeed. At times Rudge still seemed a stranger.

He closed the door with his heel and stood with his back against it, his arms held out to her. For a moment Sandra hesitated. She was a little afraid of him; or afraid of her own weakness. In the sudden silence and privacy of her little sitting room, the atmosphere was electric. If Rudge lost his self control, she was no longer sure she would be able to keep hers.

But she took that step forward into his arms almost as if it were inevitable. Rudge's arms went round her, crushing her body against him so that she gave a little cry of pain. He did not release her but put his mouth to hers and held her imprisoned against him.

'You're my girl, my girl, *my girl*!' he whispered, 'Say it, Sandie. Say you love me.'

As her arms went involuntarily round his neck, she felt a strange little moment of triumph. This was the way she wanted Rudge to be ... forgetful of all else, even his precious Mystery Man story; a little jealous, perhaps, of Bill; with no other thought in his mind but her.

Much later, when she had made tea and they were sitting arms entwined on the sofa, she herself brought up the subject of the Mystery Man, which he seemed totally to have forgotten. His grey eyes, full of laughter looked directly into hers.

'I'm glad *you* mentioned it,' he teased. 'I didn't dare!'

'Oh, shut up and tell me!' Sandie said. 'I've really been interested all along. I just didn't like you putting your sinister little story in order of first importance.'

Rudge touched a strand of Sandra's hair, twisting it idly round his finger. 'You know, darling, sinister is the right word. The police did in fact suspect murder but they simply couldn't prove anything. I was lucky enough to get on the right side of a sergeant who was on the case helping the detective. He gave me the whole story—off the record, of course. I can't quote him.'

'Well, what did he *say*?' Sandra asked impatiently.

'To start with, the body found in Baker's Pool was that of a fairly young chap. It was thought he might be a foreigner because of the pigmentation of his skin. The post mortem revealed there was extensive bruising right down one side of his head and body but at the inquest the doctor had to admit that it could have been caused by the man falling on the rocks before he went into the water. You remember, darling, how those jagged boulders jut out on the side of the pool?'

Sandra nodded. The memory of that place made her shiver. It was dark, jungle-like—just the place for a murder!

'Naturally, the first objective was to identify him,' Rudge went on. 'But although he had a wallet, a cheap plastic thing one can buy in a hundred stores all over the country, there wasn't a thing in it but a five pound note. There was a half-finished packet of cigarettes in his pocket, a sodden box of matches and that's all. No bus or train tickets. Ticket collectors and regular commuters using Ashwyck Station were all questioned as to whether they'd seen a chap like him arriving on the day of his death or during the previous days. No one had. He had no driving licence; no keys on him, so he couldn't have driven here. So the enquiries barely got off the ground. Since no one could establish where he'd come from or where he was really going to, there wasn't a base to start from.'

'What about his clothes?' Sandra asked astutely.

Rudge nodded approvingly.

'Exactly what I wanted to know, but they led nowhere, either. They were ready-made, store bought and at least two years old. The tailoring firm that mass-produced suits like the one this chap was wearing said they hadn't a hope of tracing the sale. The shirt, socks and underwear were good old M & S which, as you know, sell cash over the counter. Shoes were equally unidentifiable.'

'Teeth?' Sandra asked. 'In newspaper accounts of murders they sometimes get dentists to recognise teeth, don't they?'

Rudge sighed.

'Yes, but in this case the chap was young and only had one minor filling—could have been any dentist's handiwork. So that was that. A corpse with no name.'

'Then what were you so excited about when you picked me up at school?' Sandra asked curiously. 'Seems to me you've reached the end of the trail.'

'Well, not quite!' Rudge said, his face lighting up with renewed excitement. 'I gathered from the sergeant that the police had their eye on that artist fellow—Philip something or other—who lives in Stanfield Woods behind Baker's Pool. You must have heard about him—a kind of recluse who only leaves his hermit's cave once a month for food.'

'I did hear something about him once,' Sandra agreed, trying to search her memory for facts. 'Is he a tramp?'

'Far from it. Oxford university and public school type. The police went to see him—he's living not so far from Baker's Pool and might conceivably have heard or seen something. But apparently the chap was completely uncooperative; told them to get out and leave him alone and thoroughly put everyone's back up. They made enquiries about him but found no skeletons in his cupboard. He'd been sent down from Oxford but only because he wasn't working. His father had chucked him out of the ancestral home because he wouldn't work and disowned him when he got into debt and sold one of the family heirlooms.'

'Sounds a nasty piece of work!' Sandra commented.

'Yes, perhaps. But that doesn't make him a murderer and it didn't prove any kind of connection between him and the dead man. The police, understandably with a chap living the way he does, went into the question of whether he might be a homosexual. It could have provided a reason for the dead man, or boy, being in that part of the Stanfield Woods; it could also have provided a possible motive for murder. But they had to relinquish the idea. Judging by the fellow's paintings, he had as healthy an interest in the female body as any other normal man.'

'So that ended that lead?' Sandra prompted Rudge as he paused, lost in thought.

'Yes, it did. They put a man on to watch the cottage for a week or two but the chap never left it and no one went near the place, except . . . except Cilla Newman!' Rudge said slowly. 'It was rather odd, I thought. She told the police she was merely calling at the cottage to buy a couple of paintings. Naturally the police took her word for it though they did question the fact that she left the place empty handed. Mrs Newman explained that away by saying she hadn't seen anything she liked and didn't think Hurst was much of an artist after all.'

'So?'

'So that was that,' Rudge said doubtfully. 'But, Sandie, doesn't it seem strange to you that a woman like Cilla Newman should walk through those woods alone at six o'clock on a winter's evening—winter, mark you, so it would be pitch dark—to go and buy a painting from a man she didn't know? At least, we assume she didn't know him. From all accounts he's a surly, bad-tempered, rude individual who doesn't welcome visitors. Yet Mrs Newman, quite alone, walks through those dark woods uncertain of her welcome, to buy a picture she presumably hasn't even seen? Would *you?*'

Sandra raised her eyebrows.

'Well, no, I suppose I'd be far too scared. I'd have gone in daylight if I'd gone at all.'

'Exactly!' Rudge said triumphantly.

'But then I'm not Cilla Newman,' Sandra pointed out. 'I doubt if she would be scared of anything or anybody. I don't think its such strange behaviour, somehow, for her.'

'But it is still odd.'

'Did the police think so?'

'Apparently not. She is, after all, the wife of the local M.P. Gerald Newman was there in the room when they questioned her and he endorsed his wife's story. He'd known she was going to see Hurst, he said, and had even been a bit worried because she had not arrived home at the time she'd expected to. He'd been unaware she had been detained on her way back by the detective watching Keeper's Cottage.'

'Then there can't be anything fishy in it— not if her husband knew,' Sandie commented.

'Nevertheless, when I heard all this I had that unmistakable prickle at the back of my neck,' Rudge said with a grin that was half embarrassment. 'Call it nonsense if you want, darling, but I've learned *never* to ignore that

71

feeling when I get it. It's a sort of reporter's sixth sense. I can't explain it. I just know when I feel I'm on to something.'

'I suppose I wouldn't disregard my own "intuitions",' Sandra agreed, 'so I've no right to pooh-pooh yours. All the same, darling, don't you think you might be "wishful thinking" in this case? First you got a hunch about there being a story behind the Mystery Man. Now, though you've no real evidence of any kind to back you up, you are sort of creating a story to keep the first hunch alive.'

Rudge turned and looked directly into Sandra's eyes.

'You may be right,' he said after a moment. 'I suppose I can't expect you to back me up when, as you say, I haven't a shred of real evidence to substantiate my "feeling". But I'm going ahead anyway. I have to.'

'Going ahead with what?' Sandra asked, puzzled. 'I don't see what you can do now.'

'I'm going to call on Cilla Newman,' Rudge announced. 'If, as the police believe, she's perfectly innocent of any involvement, she won't mind talking about that evening or about her visit to Hurst. I can get some impressions from her about this chap—say I want them for my article. I can visit him, too—in fact I shall do so at the risk of being kicked out ignominiously. You can come with me if you like. Might be interesting.'

'I'm certainly not coming with you to the

Newmans' house,' Sandra said flatly. 'I can't stand Cilla Newman and I know she doesn't like me. Moreover, I'm certain she's jealous because she knows Bill likes me.'

'Then she and I have something in common,' Rudge laughed. 'Not that I see why she should concern herself with Wells' likes and dislikes—or yours, for that matter.'

It was Sandra's turn to laugh.

'You men!' she said. 'You can be very obtuse at times. She's in love with him—or at least, she's attracted to him.'

'Oh!' Rudge's one word was so full of disappointment that Sandra looked at him in surprise.

'I was hoping to establish some kind of illicit relationship between Cilla Newman and this Hurst fellow,' Rudge admitted. 'If she's after Bill Wells I'll have to scotch that idea.'

'You're being obtuse again,' Sandra said shrewdly. 'A woman like Cilla Newman could have ten lovers at the same time if she felt like it!'

'Oh ho!' Rudge said, laughing again. 'Do I detect a glimmer of cat's claws? Something tells me you don't exactly have a big opinion of our V.I.P.'s wife. Better be careful what you shout from the rooftops, my love. That last remark of yours was highly libellous.'

Sandra stood up and stretched her arms about her head, sighing.

'I'm not shouting anything from any

rooftop. I'm merely telling *you* what I *think*!' she said pointedly. 'And don't think you have a monopoly on hunches because I have a "hunch" about that woman. I wouldn't trust her a yard further than I could see her with any man.'

'Not even me?' Rudge asked, reaching up and pulling Sandra down on to his lap. 'Don't you trust me with your Gorgon, darling?'

'Least of all you!' said Sandra, giving his ear a sharp nip with her teeth.

'Stop it! And let me tell you, young woman, Cilla Newman isn't my type. For one thing I hate dyed blonde hair; for another I like my women in their twenties, not their forties, and last and by no means least . . .' he grinned . . . 'I don't go for married women. See?'

'In which case . . .' Sandra retorted, trying unsuccessfully to pull free of Rudge's arms . . . 'in which case I had better not marry you after all since you'll stop "going for me" after our wedding day . . .'

'With the exception of wives!' Rudge interrupted but Sandie's laughter made him aware of what he was suggesting.

'Enough, woman!' he told her. 'I'll argue no more with you. Kiss me and stop talking.'

The laughter was still in her eyes as she submitted eagerly to his embrace.

SIX

Rudge looked round the Newmans' drawing-room with interest. The Manor House was of Georgian period and beautiful but the furnishings as far as he had seen, lacked that aristocratic good taste usually to be found in houses of this size. Obviously a great deal of money had been spent on curtains, carpets, ornaments, but the end result just missed the elegance that he imagined the Newmans had hoped to create.

Gerald Newman had not put in an appearance as yet. It was six o'clock and Rudge had supposed he would be at home. When he rang Cilla Newman to ask if he might come and interview her, Cilla had sounded vaguely amused.

'What on earth about?' she had asked in that hard brittle voice of hers. 'Politics, I suppose,' she added without waiting for his reply. 'Well there's no reason why not. Come at six and we'll have drinks. Gerald will probably be around, too.'

She came into the drawing-room now, looking slim and in Rudge's eyes, not unattractive in a short tight-fitting black dress. She approached him with a questioning smile on her carefully made-up face.

'Sorry to keep you waiting, Mr Rudgely.

75

Let me get you a drink. Sherry? Gin? Whisky? You name it, we have it.'

'I'll have a gin and tonic, please.'

Rudge watched as she poured herself a generous brandy. She was obviously a drinking woman. It showed in her face which Rudge could not help comparing unfavourably with Sandra's.

'Well?' Cilla asked as they sat opposite one another. 'I'm more than a little curious to know what you wish to interview me about. Or is it Gerald you want to talk to? Don't tell me my dear brother-in-law has decided to feature wives in his paper for a change?'

Rudge had almost forgotten that his editor and Gerald Newman were brothers, although of course he was well aware of the relationship. But the two men were so unalike both in looks and appearance, one tended not to think of them as close relatives.

'As a matter of fact, Mr Newman—Mr Frank Newman—doesn't know I'm here and probably wouldn't be a bit pleased if he did!' Rudge admitted. 'I hope you won't throw me out?'

To his relief, Cilla laughed.

'On the contrary, I'm even more intrigued. Frank's a stodgy old fool, in my opinion, and the *Stanfield Observer* a deadly bore. If you're going to breathe some fresh air into the paper, I'm right with you.'

She smiled at him provocatively over the

rim of her glass. Rudge relaxed. He hadn't been too sure of his reception. Now it was obvious that not only was this woman open to a little flattery, but she was quite prepared to indulge in a mild flirtation. He knew her reputation in Ashwyck; knew, too, that she seemed to have a penchant for younger men. But he had imagined since she was currently interested in Bill Wells that she wouldn't have time for anyone else. Now he had the strongest intuition that given a few more drinks, the 'interview' could develop into something very different—if he were interested, which, of course he was not. This woman was not his type. Besides which, there was Sandie.

He accepted the cigarette she offered him and when he had lit it, he began to explain about his interest in the Mystery Man's grave; how it had led him to Philip Hurst and finally to her. Watching her face as he spoke, he was aware that he held more than her casual interest—she seemed totally fascinated by what he was saying. Her eyes never left his face. When he finally stopped speaking, she continued to stare at him as if mesmerised.

'You are one of the few people in Ashwyck who could give me a first-hand assessment of Philip Hurst,' he said. 'That's what I came for!'

The woman opposite him stood up so suddenly, she spilled the last of her brandy on the green Wilton carpet. It soaked into the pile but she either did not notice or did not care for she made no move to wipe it up. Instead she walked across to the table and poured herself another drink. Her back towards him, she said coldly:

'I really don't see why you should imagine *I* can tell you anything about the man. As to his having any connection with the murder—if it *was* a murder—I doubt it very much. Frankly, Mr Rudgely, I have to agree with my brother-in-law. You're wasting your time. That old ten days' wonder has become nothing but a deadly bore. I cannot see what point there is in going into it again after all these years. Besides, if the police decided the case should be closed, what makes you think *you* can find out anything they couldn't at the time?'

He was surprised into silence. Her words were completely opposite to the avid interest she had shown a moment earlier. It didn't make sense. If she really thought the whole subject so boring, what had caused her to listen to him, eyes widened, lips parted, as if she didn't want to miss a word he was saying? This last reaction was discouraging to say the least of it. No one had shown any enthusiasm for his 'hunch' and he had thought that at last he had found if not an ally, at least someone who was interested enough to encourage him to probe deeper into the story. But far from it. Cilla Newman was rejecting the idea as forcefully as his editor had done.

'Perhaps *you* find the subject boring,' he conceded as politely as he could. 'But I'm more or less a newcomer to Ashwyck and frankly, I'm intrigued by what happened. It isn't often a reporter like myself comes upon an unsolved murder at such close quarters.'

'If it *was* murder!' Cilla broke in sharply. 'It could just as easily have been an accident. Really, Mr Rudgely, you aren't a detective. I should have thought matters of this kind were outside your sphere.'

Rudge hid a smile. If Cilla Newman thought to put him off by that cold, derogatory tone of voice, she was much mistaken. His hide was fairly tough. He could take a lot worse than a woman like her could deal out.

'I've always found crime fascinating,' he said easily. 'And despite what you have just said, Mrs Newman, and what the police think, *I* think a crime was committed at Baker's Pool—not an accident.'

'What makes you think so?' his companion replied sharply. 'You haven't a shred of evidence to support your theory. *Or have you?*'

Rudge shrugged his shoulders.

'No, not evidence—just a hunch. Perhaps I'm wrong—but I mean to follow it up, even if I'm proved wrong in the end. You can help me if you want to. I need to know more about Philip Hurst.'

Cilla walked across the room and with her back still to Rudge, stood staring out of the window.

'I'm afraid I can't enlighten you about Hurst. I once nearly bought a couple of pictures from him and that's the extent of my association with him.'

Rudge felt the hair prickle in the nape of his neck. He had the strongest impression that she was lying to him. He would have liked to see her face but she seemed determined to keep her back to him.

'All the same, you must be able to give me some idea of what the man is like. A woman can usually sum up a man even on the briefest acquaintance.'

Now she did turn and look at him. Her eyes were narrowed thoughtfully.

'Well of course, I formed *some* impressions—but I'm afraid they won't be of the slightest use to you, Mr Rudgely. I thought him a bad painter and a rude, unsociable, introverted kind of man. I would doubt very much indeed that he had sufficient interest in any of his fellow men to take the trouble or the risks involved in murdering one of them. Does that satisfy you?'

Rudge put down his empty glass.

'It interests me,' he said thoughtfully, 'but it merely confirms what the police have to say about him. I'd rather hoped you could give me a more personal angle, Mrs Newman.'

Did he imagine it or had she really paled as he spoke?

'Personal? What do you mean?'

'I'd simply like to know what you sensed. For instance, would you say he was interested in women? Surely you would know that. I thought women could always feel these things.'

Cilla's mouth curled.

'I really don't see why I should bother to answer your rather impertinent questions, Mr Rudgely. I doubt if my brother-in-law would be any too pleased to learn that you'd taken it upon yourself to cross-question me.'

Rudge felt an inexplicable moment of triumph. If Cilla was entirely innocent of any closer association with Hurst, there would be no reason for her to resent his questions. The fact that she was really threatening him with his editor's disapproval indicated to him that she was on the defensive.

'Of course you aren't under any obligation to reply,' he said smoothly. 'Though for the life of me, I can't see why you should mind doing so. After all, it isn't as if you had anything to hide, is it?'

He could see from her widened eyes that his shot had gone home. She paused fractionally and then let her face relax into a smile.

'Of course not! I don't in the least mind answering questions, Mr Rudgely. I merely find the subject matter somewhat boring, as I said before. I scarcely know Philip Hurst, and I doubt if anyone else in Ashwyck knows much about him either. He keeps very much to himself—leads a sort of hermit-like existence at Keeper's Cottage. If he did, in fact, have anything to do with the man who was drowned in Baker's Pool, then he must have covered his tracks very efficiently, otherwise the police would have associated him with the crime, wouldn't they? So you are merely wasting your time—and mine—trying to probe into Philip Hurst's private life.'

Rudge admired the logic of her reply but he still had that tingling sensation that she was withholding information. He had found in the course of many years interviewing people, that he could feel—with almost a physical sensation—whether they were speaking the truth or not and whether he was being given the facts or merely told what the interviewed person wished him to know.

He decided to try shock treatment—often effective in cases like this where straight questions were being parried.

'Of course, the man's clearly a homosexual!' he stated suddenly.

'That's ridiculous. He . . .' She broke off but could not retract the instant denial that had escaped her in that one unguarded moment. Rudge had his answer and they both knew it.

'Most of his paintings are of women,' Cilla

tried to extricate herself with a skill Rudge had to admire. 'That's why I'm absolutely certain your suggestion is absurd.'

'I don't think the fact that he paints women rather than men proves anything,' Rudge said, hoping she would be put off guard by his apparent naïvety.

Cilla shot him a quick glance.

'Don't you? Well, if it'll help you to straighten yourself out, I'll tell you off the record that he tried to make a pass at me. So you see, Mr Rudgely, you're on the wrong lines. Take my advice and stop dabbling in matters that are really outside your scope.'

Rudge stood up. He was momentarily satisfied. He already had one fact the police were not aware of. He decided to pretend a sudden loss of confidence in himself; and to re-establish a friendly contact with Cilla.

'I expect you must be thinking I'm a bit of a fool,' he said with what he hoped was an apologetic smile. 'But I rather got carried away with my own wild ideas about the Mystery Man. It's the kind of thing every young reporter dreams about—solving the unsolvable crime and having the Big Exclusive. You do understand?'

For a moment Cilla hesitated. She was by no means sure that Rudge was as innocent as he was making out. Sensing her uncertainty, he added:

'I had the crazy notion that if I could prove

Philip Hurst was a homosexual the unknown man might easily be blackmailing him. You can see what I'm getting at, can't you? Hurst hides away in the wilds, this former acquaintance finds him and starts asking for money so Hurst pushes him into Baker's Pool. It would provide a motive for the murder as well as explaining why no one in Ashwyck could identify the body.'

Cilla, he could see, was listening attentively. He half expected her to encourage him in this hypothetical line of thought. It would keep suspicion of an association between her and Hurst at bay if he really did believe it. But Cilla was shaking her head.

'I'm sure you are wrong, Mr Rudgely. Philip Hurst may be a bit of an eccentric but as I said before, I don't think he has any connection with the accident. I really do suggest most strongly that you stop letting your imagination run away with you in this . . . forgive me if I sound patronising . . . in this rather naïve way. Frank, my brother-in-law, is an astute man. If he has told you he doesn't want time wasted on this story, then if I were you I'd take his word for it that there's nothing more to be written about it. Surely, Mr Rudgely, you have better things to do with your spare time?'

She came across to him and touched his arm lightly in a gesture that could have been innocent but which equally he could have taken as an invitation. She smiled and said huskily:

'It would be a pity if you and I couldn't be friends. I'm afraid I was a bit rough on you just now but really I didn't mean to be unfriendly. Am I forgiven?'

The charm was turned on full force. Rudge decided to play along. He didn't want her contacting Newman and getting him fired. If he allowed her to think she was exerting some influence over him he would be in a far stronger position than if he antagonised her. He covered the hand on his arm with his own and said:

'I'm the one to be forgiven—barging in here and expecting you to answer a lot of silly questions. I must have bored you, I'm afraid, Mrs Newman.'

'I'd like it much better if you called me Cilla. Now, let me get you another drink— Bob isn't it? Christian names are so much pleasanter. Gerald should be along soon. I know he'd like to meet you. It's really very silly we haven't met before, socially— although, of course, I *have* noticed you at the Golf Club. We must have a game sometime.'

'I'm afraid you'd be rather above my standard,' Rudge replied. 'I've heard you play off eight, and you won the Ladies' Championship last summer, didn't you?'

They discussed golf in an easy, relaxed way until Gerald came in. He let Cilla introduce

Rudge and then said curtly:

'I don't want to appear rude, Rudgely, but my wife and I are dining out. I'm afraid . . .'

'That's all right—I was just leaving,' Rudge interrupted. He wondered if Gerald's excuse to be rid of him was genuine. Somehow, he doubted it. He turned to Cilla to thank her profusely for making him so welcome. She gave him a meaningful glance.

'You must come to dinner soon. I'll arrange something. Now we've established contact, we mustn't lose touch.'

'Of course not,' Rudge agreed easily, holding her hand a trifle longer than was necessary. 'Maybe I can take you up on that game of golf, too. Good night, Mrs Newman—Mr Newman.'

Outside the house, Rudge stood for a moment breathing in the fresh evening air. He was eating with Sandie at the Waterman's Arms and already he was half an hour late. He knew he should hurry but he walked slowly across the gravel drive to his car, lost in thought. One fact had emerged clearly from this hour he had spent with Cilla Newman— he was quite convinced that she was involved in some way with Philip Hurst. His next move was to see the man himself. This might not be easy. From the police sergeant's account, Hurst was liable to slam the front door in his face if he called. But if he were to use Cilla Newman's name . . .

Thoughtfully, Rudge climbed into his car and pulled the door shut. It had been an interesting hour, he reflected. Not that he'd achieved much in relation to his Mystery Man story. Even were he able to prove that Cilla Newman had been having an affair with Philip Hurst, he was no nearer finding a link between them and the man who had drowned. Nor would he be any nearer identifying the unknown man or supplying a motive for his murder—if it was murder. Really and truly, he had discovered nothing to account for this tense feeling of excitement as if he were on the brink of something important.

He turned out of the drive and headed back towards the pub. To get there, he had to cross the bridge over the culvert that spilled water into Baker's Pool. He drove slowly, letting his strange fantasies play around in his mind. There *had* to be an explanation. There had been a body and the body must have had an identity; must have had a reason for being here on this bridge or beside the pool. Not a fisherman because he had no tackle. Just someone—but who? And why? And was it simply Philip Hurst's bad luck that he happened to be the only person living anywhere near the scene of the crime—if it was a crime!

Rudge sighed. He knew that most people would think him quite mad to waste so much valuable time and thought on a mere 'hunch'.

Even Sandra wasn't enthusiastic and if she didn't understand how he felt, who else would? Everyone seemed bent on discouraging him from pursuing a 'dead' story; Frank Newman, the police, Cilla Newman. Yet he had to go on probing—no matter how crazy it might seem even to himself!

He drove into the pub car park, suddenly once more conscious of time. Sandra would have been waiting over an hour for him—if she *was* still waiting. The chances were she'd be pretty annoyed. In a way, he wouldn't blame her. It wasn't going to be easy to explain why he had *had* to stay so long with Cilla Newman. It might be simpler not to explain at all.

He walked into the lounge bar and one look at Sandie's face decided him on the latter course of behaviour.

'Why . . . ?' he asked himself ruefully, 'did women—especially adorable, pretty girls like Sandie White—have to make life so complicated for a man?'

'Darling!' he said, bending to kiss her averted cheek. 'I'm so sorry to have kept you waiting. Let me get you a drink.'

'No thanks!' said Sandie coldly. 'Not until you've explained why I have had to sit here alone for the best part of an hour. Work, I suppose. Well, it had better not be that blasted Mystery Man story or I'm going straight home.'

He stood staring down at her, mesmerised in part by the stunning attraction of her flashing blue eyes—and in part by his own acute dismay.

SEVEN

'That's why I came this evening.' Cilla Newman ended her account of her meeting with Bob Rudgely. 'To put you on your guard!'

Philip Hurst did not answer her. He continued to apply paint to the canvas in front of him, smearing it with his right thumb. His dark brows, flecked with grey, were drawn together in concentration. As far as the woman could see, his expression had remained unchanged since she had begun speaking to him. For all she knew, he may not have heard her at all. His mouth was a thin, tight line; the nose above aquiline. He was unshaven and had obviously trimmed his small pointed beard himself.

Cilla grimaced. The man in front of her had ceased to have any attraction at all for her. She found him, on the contrary, slightly repulsive.

She thought, not without a trace of wry amusement, that it would be easy to imagine, if you were Bob Rudgely, that this man was capable of murder. Suddenly, she shivered, pulling the cyclamen mohair wool cardigan closer about her neck and shoulders. There was little warmth in the thin silk dress she wore and the evening was cool now that the sun had gone down.

'Did you hear me, Philip?' she said sharply.

The man picked up a long-handled paint brush and chewed the end between large, surprisingly white teeth. His eyes had not turned from his painting—a not very effective self-portrait, recognisable only because of the hair and eye colouring and the similarity of clothes. It was not good, Cilla thought, but then none of his paintings were.

'I heard you,' he said at last. He turned then and gave her a grimace which could have passed for a smile in that thin, bitter visage. 'I was thinking that your warning was a little inappropriate. Surely you are the one who should be on guard?'

Cilla flushed. Philip had a maddening aptitude for striking where it hurt most. She snapped open her handbag and pulled out a cigarette packet. When she had selected one, she tapped it angrily on the back of the packet before inserting it between her lips. The action steadied her rising anger.

'Naturally I am looking out for myself!' she said coldly. 'So I'll save you the trouble of saying the obvious. But Rudgely means to question you. *We must tell the same story, Philip.*'

The man put down the paint brush and

began to wipe his hands methodically on a filthy paint rag. When this was done to his satisfaction, and regardless of Cilla's mounting impatience he took his time about it, then only did he go across the room he used as his studio to pour out two whiskys from the bottle on the table. He handed one to Cilla and watched her drink deeply from the glass.

'You *are* nervous!' he commented shrewdly. 'Have you been telling the young man lots of lies, my dear?'

'Lots!' Cilla said bluntly. 'For one thing, you and I have only met on one occasion—the evening I was stopped by the detective leaving here. Otherwise we know nothing about each other. It's in your interest as well as mine . . .' she added sharply . . . 'to bear out that story, Philip. If Rudgely once gets the idea I've been lying, there'll be no end to the questions. You've got to stop this idea he has that you are connected with the murder.'

The man seemed to take her remarks unperturbed.

'My dear girl,' he said coldly, 'how could he possibly *prove* any such thing.' He stressed the one word. 'If the police couldn't at the time, he certainly won't be able to prove anything after all these years.'

Cilla drained the whisky from her glass and handed it to Philip for a refill. His calmness was beginning to have an effect, along with the alcohol. She no longer felt so panicky as she had when Rudgely left the house and she'd felt impelled to rush here and warn Philip.

'All the same, he could make things very awkward for me if he finds out about us . . .' she said as much to herself as to Philip.

'Then isn't it a little indiscreet of you to come here this evening?'

Cilla stubbed out her cigarette angrily.

'Okay, so it was risky. But I had to let you know he would be coming to see you. Probably tomorrow morning, I guess. Since you refuse to be on the telephone how else could I contact you except by coming here?'

'You could have written a letter.'

'No!' Cilla interrupted. 'How could I possibly put such things in writing. In this village, a letter could easily get into the wrong hands and . . .'

She broke off, suddenly uneasy. Blackmail was hardly a word to mention to a blackmailer. Watching her face, Philip suddenly laughed. There was no humour in the sound—only cruelty. She knew he had accurately guessed her thoughts.

'I despise you, Philip Hurst!' she said fiercely. 'I despise you more than any man I know. You disgust me. I . . .'

She broke off as he came towards her, putting down his whisky glass as he approached, eyebrows raised in mock amusement.

'And you're afraid of me!' he finished for her, as he pulled her roughly to her feet and encircled her waist with his hands. He held her for a moment in front of him, staring down into her eyes with the same mesmeristic hypnotic stare of a snake. She shivered, trying to pull free of his grip but he tightened his hold on her and bent suddenly to kiss her neck.

'Let me go, Philip!' Her words were more a cry of appeal than a demand but he ignored them and began to kiss her savagely. 'Let me go!' she begged once more but he only laughed.

'I think I find your resistance even more stimulating than your acquiescence,' he said. 'There is a certain sadistic satisfaction for me in overcoming your objections with force. Strange, my dear, that we should have come full circle like this! Remember our first encounter? You fought quite hard then, didn't you? But not since . . . not until lately. I wonder what has brought about the change in your reactions? You used to be so avid for sex, didn't you?'

He turned his face quickly sideways to avoid the blow she tried to strike. He gave her no second opportunity, catching her hands and pinning them behind her back. He was immeasurably stronger than she.

'Another man, perhaps?' he taunted, and seeing the colour flare into her cheeks,

93

laughed again. 'So I guessed right. Well, my dear, I'm afraid *he* will have to make do with my left-overs. I haven't the slightest intention of handing you over on a platter for him to enjoy. From now on, Cilla, I will expect you here once a week. Understand?'

'I won't!' she gasped out between clenched teeth. 'Let me go. You're hurting me.'

He gave her a sudden push backwards so that she fell on to the sofa behind them. Then he stood looking down at her, his eyes travelling over her body. Her short skirt was caught up beneath her in her fall so that the long slim legs were fully exposed. His eyes narrowed.

'You're surprisingly attractive—for a woman of your age!' he said brutally.

He made love to her fiercely, selfishly, like some wild beast. There was no attempt this time to ensure that she should find the same enjoyment from the encounter. It was as if he were trying to prove his complete mastery over her. Though she clawed at him with her nails and writhed and struggled, she was at all times powerless to escape from the inevitable.

'I hate you!' she gasped when at last he let go. 'I'll never come here again. You . . . you *hurt* me!' she was nearly crying with rage and humiliation, the more aggravated because she knew very well that her threats were meaningless. She had to obey him. To go against him was to jeopardise her whole life.

94

They both knew it. It was another form of blackmail—the price she had to pay for Philip's silence.

She lay suddenly quiet, wordless, watching him as he stood up. One day, somehow, she would be revenged. The time would come—*must* come, when she'd make him pay for this last half hour, and for all the other torment he had inflicted on her. But common sense, returning now that she was safe from any further assault, warned her that this wasn't the right moment to make an enemy of him. She was doubly dependent upon him now that stupid young reporter had started nosing into the past.

Philip had returned to his easel. He was painting silently, calmly, as if there had been no interval between now and her arrival half an hour earlier. Cilla watched him, frowning a little as she tried to fathom him out. Was he really as devoid of human feelings as he appeared? Could any man become so embittered with the human race that they could withdraw as completely as Philip seemed to have done? The ordinary decent traits were missing in him—there was no gentleness, no tenderness, sympathy, understanding, generosity, no capacity for love.

Was a man born this way, handicapped from birth, or could life make a normal, decent child into a cruel, sadistic, egotistical man she wondered? Could he ever have been otherwise? It was impossible to know. Perhaps a psychiatrist could discover the answer but certainly she could not. She merely knew that Philip was different from other men. That very difference had at first attracted her and then, eventually, repelled her. She wished more desperately than ever before that she could be free of him. Yet he was part of her life now, as inescapably as if steel handcuffs chained them together.

She shivered and standing up, went across the room to pour herself a stiff drink. Philip did not turn from his painting. She might not have existed for all the acknowledgment he gave of her presence in the room.

The drink steadied her. She went over and stood behind Philip, staring over his arm at the painting. It still seemed as bad a portrait as she'd thought on seeing it for the first time. The contours of the face were stiff, amateurish, without life or likeness. Yet he was applying paint with the concentration of a man utterly dedicated to his talent. Did he really believe himself gifted? Did he hope in his secret heart—if he had one—that one day he would be recognised as a second Michelangelo or Picasso? He must believe he was good for him to spend his whole life painting the way he did. Had no one ever disillusioned him?

'You've never thought of exhibiting,

Philip?' she asked suddenly, breaking the silence that lay heavily over the room.

He did not turn his head, but a faint cynical smile twisted the corners of his mouth.

'No!' he answered curtly. 'I don't need fame!'

'Nor money!' Cilla added bitterly, moving away from him with a renewed feeling of revulsion.

Philip gave a sudden harsh laugh.

'Sometimes, my dear Cilla, listening to you, I have the impression you think yourself a paragon of all the virtues. That *you* should sit in judgement on me causes me not a little amusement. Do you really believe you are a better person than I?'

She clenched her teeth furiously. His barb stung. She was no plaster saint and she knew it.

'Nevertheless, I wouldn't stoop to blackmail!' she spat out the words.

'How conventional you are, my dear! Society may condemn blackmail as a dastardly crime but personally, I do not. I see no reason why those who have committed other, perhaps worse crimes and remained undetected, should not pay for their sins. That I should be the recipient of those payments— and mark you, my victim can very well *afford* what I ask—seems to me to be perfectly fair. Why should I offer my silence for free? I owe him nothing. I see no reason at all why he

97

shouldn't keep me in moderate comfort while he continues to live in the first place, a free man, and in the second place, in considerably more comfort than *I* derive from *him*. I've never increased my demands from my original agreement. I don't "put on the screw". He knows exactly where he stands just as I do. Keeping me supplied with the means of livelihood is no more to him than keeping any other dependant. You can scarcely call me extravagant.'

'You may justify your actions to yourself, Philip, but you can't justify them to me nor could you to a jury. If it was ever found out . . .'

'But it will not be, Cilla!' Philip broke in quietly. 'It is not in either of our interests to betray the other. You, for instance, took the trouble—and the risk—to come and warn me to be discreet! No, my dear, no one is going to upset our very satisfactory and private arrangement.'

His words reminded her that she had already spent far too long at the cottage. Darkness had fallen and she had more than a mile to walk through the woods. As Philip had said, there was a certain risk involved in coming here. Although it was very seldom indeed anyone used the cart track to Keeper's Cottage, nevertheless occasionally a courting couple or even a poacher after pheasants or rabbits, might choose the same moment as she to be out in the dark. It would be difficult to explain her presence at this time, alone . . .

'Shut the door as you go!' Philip said, still not turning from his work. 'And don't forget, I'll expect you back next week.'

She did not reply, anger choking the retort she would have liked to make. If she could only be free to tell him she never intended seeing him again, if . . .

She shut the door behind her and switching on her torch, began her lonely and none too pleasant journey home.

EIGHT

'I thought I told you I wanted you to drop this story?'

Rudge looked across the desk at his editor's white, furious face with a sense of shock. It wasn't so surprising that Frank Newman knew he was still pursuing his Mystery Man story; he'd more or less expected Cilla Newman would pass on the information. What did surprise him was the violence of his editor's reaction.

'Look here, sir, what I do in my spare time is surely my own affair . . .' he began but Newman interrupted him:

'You represent this paper, Rudgely. You used your influence as our reporter to get into my sister-in-law's home and bother her with a

99

whole lot of absurd questions. I won't have it, do you understand?'

Rudge moved away from the desk and the angry gaze of the older man's eyes. So it *was* Cilla Newman who had complained to her brother-in-law.

'You're to drop the story as from now. That's an order!' Rudge did not reply. He simply could not make out why his editor should be so adamant—no, it was more even than that—it was almost threatening. He felt his own quick temper rising.

'And if I don't?' he asked quietly, turning back to face his companion, his grey eyes as angry now as the other's.

'Then I shall be forced to interpret your refusal as a direct disobedience to my orders,' Frank Newman said warningly. 'I don't want to have to ask you to find another job, Rudgely . . .' his tone had become more conciliatory . . . 'You and I have got along very well together until now and I don't mind admitting that I think very highly indeed of a lot of the work you do for us. It was my intention, as you know, to take things a bit easier in the near future and to leave a lot of the responsibility for the *Observer* in your hands. I haven't told you this but I've been looking for a junior reporter to take over some of the less interesting work you do to leave you free to understudy me. I hoped, eventually, to train you to take over from me.

It would be most distressing to me, at this stage, to have to reconsider my plans.'

Rudge felt a little of the tenseness leave his muscles. He knew deep down that Newman liked him; that he really meant to help him up to the editor's chair. It was all the more puzzling, therefore, to hear the old boy actually threaten dismissal—for that's what he'd done—just because he wished to pursue his own story in his own time. It didn't make sense.

'Look, Mr Newman, I appreciate all you have done for me and equally what you intend doing for me. I like my job here and I like working for you. As a matter of fact, I was a bit of a rolling stone when I first came to Ashwyck; I wasn't too sure I would settle. But now I'm unofficially engaged and intending to get married and it suits my purpose to have a steady job I like where the prospects are good. I don't *want* to leave. But there's something in my make-up that resents bitterly anything savouring of injustice. Frankly, I cannot see what right you have or anyone else has, come to that, to control what I do in my own time. Perhaps I should have explained to Mrs Gerald Newman exactly why I wanted to see her. I am prepared to accept that I traded a little on my position as your reporter—not that I said so but my lack of any other explanation may have implied so. For this I apologise. I hadn't the slightest wish to make a nuisance of myself and Mrs Newman wasn't forced or harried into answering any questions if she did not wish to do so. However, none of this affects the point at issue—namely that I should be free to do as I please in my own time.'

The older man surprised Rudge by making no attempt to interrupt his fairly lengthy speech. His anger seemed to have cooled and he relaxed in his chair, toying with a pencil as if lost in thought. When he spoke, he sounded more weary than annoyed.

'Of course your free time is your own, Rudgely. I didn't mean to imply otherwise. I'm merely telling you I want you to drop this ridiculous enquiry of yours into an accident that happened three years ago. You are a reporter, not a detective, and even if you were to discover the name of the drowned man, I shouldn't print the facts in the Observer. People aren't interested in ancient news, as you should very well know.'

Rudge's mouth tightened. 'I don't entirely agree with you, sir. Murder is always news and a murder discovered three years after is often even more newsworthy.'

'It was not a murder!' Frank Newman burst out with a renewal of anger.

'Not proven, I agree,' Rudge sought to remain calm. 'But I'm more than ever sure in my own mind that it was. Whether you ultimately prove me wrong and whether or not you ultimately print the story, I want to find out the truth for my own satisfaction. Is there anything wrong in that?'

Newman swore softly under his breath as the pencil he was holding snapped in his fingers. He threw the pieces into the waste paper basket and clasped his hands together on top of the pile of page proofs on his desk.

"There's nothing wrong, Rudgely. I merely don't wish you to waste your time on such an absurd fantasy. My sister-in-law told me you intended visiting Philip Hurst presumably to ask more questions. Well, you won't get anything out of him and you'll leave with a considerable sized flea in your ear for your trouble. I can tell you anything you want to know about him.'

'I'd rather find out for myself,' Rudge said stubbornly.

'Don't be so childish, Rudgely!' Newman was beginning to lose his temper again. 'If you go on this way, you will end up antagonising all the residents of Ashwyck. Then, when we do need their co-operation for some worthwhile story, we won't get it. Now do you see why I want you to drop this notion here and now. You weren't here at the time of the ... the accident. I was. A lot of unpleasantness was stirred up at the time. You know how people in a small village gossip, and for the brief while the murder was being investigated, everyone was suspicious of their neighbour. It made everyday life very unpleasant and I've no wish to revive those feelings. They took quite a time to die down even after the police had closed the files. Oblige me now by letting sleeping dogs lie.'

'And if I don't?'

The older man met Rudge's eyes with a long, cold stare. 'If you don't, Rudgely, I shall be forced to assume that you put your own judgement before mine. As your employer, I should naturally not enjoy that assumption.' As if suddenly aware that the young man in front of him was likely to be stiffened in his resolve by threats, he added a quiet appeal:

'If you had experienced some of the beastliness that erupted over that case, you wouldn't be so anxious to stir up the mud,' he said, as much to himself as to Rudge. 'There were the usual crop of poison-pen letters—people with chips on their shoulders anxious to cast suspicion on someone they resented or thought they had a grudge against. There were men put in Coventry by suspicious workmates; housewives gossiping over hedges and not confining their gossip to the case in hand. There was even a suicide . . . a middle-aged biology master at the school. The poor devil had a bit of a past—been suspected of assaulting a boy at his previous school. Nothing had been proved against him and his record was clean. He'd settled here and there was nothing likely to associate him with the past—until the accident. He was afraid the police would make their routine enquiries about him and the facts about his past catch up with him. So he killed himself. For nothing, as it happened. The police only learned the facts from his farewell note. So you see, Rudgely, the kind of thing that can happen when there is suspicion without proof.'

Rudge was silent. Newman had made a point. He hadn't known about the suicide because the files had been missing . . .

'Who did take the files?' he asked suddenly. 'And why?' The older man did not reply at once. Rudge was not sure for a moment if he had heard his question. But eventually he said softly:

'I took them, Rudgely. They were, after all, my property. Perhaps I had some foreknowledge that someone like yourself would start probing into the past. I wanted to avoid such a thing happening. As a matter of fact, I knew that biology master, Roderick Byers, quite well. We used to play chess together. I liked him. His death was a great shock to me. Even now I sometimes find myself thinking about it—regretting the needless waste of a life. He was a good man, despite that one lapse. He'd more than paid the price for it and was making good when . . . well, Rudgely, there's no point going into it further. I've answered your questions and I trust you are now in agreement with me. Drop the story, there's a good fellow.'

It would have been easy enough to say 'yes'. Rudge was fair-minded and Newman had made his point well. There was no real justification for what he, Rudge, was doing. Nevertheless, he wasn't sure he could stop probing now. Too many nerve ends were alerted. He wouldn't be able to sleep at night for wondering whether, if he went a step or two further, he'd uncover something vital . . .

'May I think about it, sir?' he prevaricated. 'I'd like to fall in with your wishes but . . . well, can I think it over?'

Newman gave him a long hard look.

'I shan't change my mind, Rudgely. If you go against me in this, you're out. You understand?'

Rudge nodded.

But once outside Newman's office, he wasn't so sure he did understand. Newman must feel extraordinarily deeply to make such an ultimatum. The man must know very well that Rudge wasn't in any way trying to challenge his authority. When Newman had suggested such a thing, it had seemed a plausible reason for threatening to sack him. But on reflection, it was far from plausible. It was a personal, not an office matter.

Not altogether to his surprise but to his intense annoyance, Sandra, in whom he had confided at lunch, sided with Newman.

'I agree with him entirely,' she said. 'I didn't know about the suicide—obviously the school kept a thing like that quiet—but if raking up an old case could lead to more of that kind of thing, then I'm agin it.'

Rudge frowned.

'You can't go through life being an ostrich, Sandie,' he said forcefully. 'Pretending something isn't there won't make it go away. This could have been murder—*murder!*' he repeated. 'Just for a moment, accept that it was. So somewhere walking around is the murderer, yes? They could murder a second time—perhaps already have done so. So what right have you, or has Newman or anyone else to say: "Leave well alone". On the contrary, I think it's our moral duty to find out the truth.'

'No matter who gets hurt in the process?' Sandie asked with more feeling behind the words than perhaps she had intended.

'The innocent shouldn't get hurt,' Rudge retorted sharply.

'But it does happen—you know it does. And then there's another point to consider, Rudge. You asked me to suppose it was murder. Now I ask you to suppose it wasn't. If it *was* an accident, what possible excuse have you for upsetting everyone just to satisfy your own morbid curiosity?'

'It isn't morbid and it isn't curiosity,' Rudge took up the cudgels violently.

'Then what is it?' Sandie asked bitterly. 'Do

you realise that you and I have done nothing but quarrel ever since you started this wild goose chase? You're obsessed with it. You can't think of anything else—even me. Well, I meant what I said last night when you kept me waiting alone for a whole hour while you cross-questioned Cilla Newman—it isn't my idea of how a man newly engaged to a girl should behave. I've a right, surely, to some of your time, your consideration? The day before yesterday, you cut our lunch. Today, we talk of nothing else through lunch. What about *us*, Rudge? Don't we matter?'

'Darling, yes, of course!' Rudge said, softening at once to the appeal in her blue eyes. 'But you must be fair—at the beginning you were as interested as I. It was something we were going to do together. Then suddenly you drop out—go all disapproving. Why?'

Sandra sighed.

'I suppose because you're letting it matter more than anything else in your life. You've lost your sense of proportion, Rudge. It's only a story—and a pretty vague one at that. Yet you behave as if you're on the brink of putting a man on the moon! Why, you sit there and tell me quite calmly as if it weren't in the least important that you may go ahead at the cost of your job. Did you mean that?'

Rudge nodded.

'There you are, then!' Sandra said triumphantly. 'It shows how little I mean by comparison. We're engaged to be married, remember? We should be saving hard now so that we can afford our own home. My flat's fine for just the two of us, but one day when we have a family, we'll want our own house. How are we going to put anything by for the future if you're going to throw your job up every time you aren't allowed to follow up one of your "hunches"?'

She hadn't meant to say any of those things. They had all been in the back of her mind but when she opened her mouth to speak, she had had no intention of saying them. They sounded possessive, nagging, housewifely—all the things she'd hoped never to be! Now she felt an added resentment against Rudge for making her like that. He should be the one to be planning for their future—telling her he couldn't possibly throw up his job now they were getting married. Then she might have reacted very differently, telling him he must do what he felt right regardless of her!

'I'm sorry you feel this way,' Rudge was saying. 'I must say I never expected it from you, Sandie. I thought you understood—about my work, I mean.'

'I do!' Sandie nearly burst out but she bit back the words. Why should she make things easy for Rudge. If he didn't start to consider her now before their marriage, what kind of life would it be after? He'd always maintained he believed in equality, the emancipation of women. Then let him prove it. She had as much right to say how she felt and what she wanted as he did.

Rudge drained his coffee cup and replacing it in the saucer, pushed it away from him with unseeing eyes. He seemed lost in thought. The silence between them became long drawn out until it was painfully obvious to them both that one or the other must break it. Sandie wanted to. She realised that Rudge was waiting for her to show a little sympathy and understanding. She knew he was seriously concerned about his discussion this morning with his editor; that his self-confidence had been shaken. He wanted her to back him up—and she wouldn't. Not because she cared much one way or the other about the story but because . . . because . . . she didn't really know why.

Rudge, in his turn, wanted desperately to put things right between them. He realised that he'd upset Sandie by not seeming to care enough about her. But it was so ridiculous. He loved her desperately and she must know it. It was ridiculous to make out that he'd behaved as if he didn't. Why, he'd come straight to her following his talk with Newman, desperately needing her backing, her belief in him. If anyone was showing a lack of love and understanding, it was Sandie!

'So you're joining the ranks of the enemy?' he said at last, his voice bitter with hurt pride.

'Don't be so dramatic, Rudge!' was her curt reply. 'You really are being childish about the whole thing. No wonder Frank Newman is fed up. I would be in his shoes. To hear you talk, you'd think he was personally anxious to do you down in some way.'

'And to hear you talk, you obviously approve of him trying to curtail my freedom to do as I think fit. Thanks for your loyalty, Sandra. Another time, I'll know better than to count on it.'

Sandra felt as if he had struck her. In fact, his words had struck at her own vague guilty feeling that she was letting him down. It was horrible to realise that they were really quarrelling now for the first time in their lives—not just a mild disagreement in general discussion, but a real quarrel. She wanted desperately to end it—to say she was sorry; to see Rudge's face soften and fill with love again. But her pride wouldn't permit her to do what she wanted. She did not believe, for one thing, that she was altogether in the wrong. Rudge had brought a lot of this on himself by being so single-minded about his wretched story. He thought of nothing else—and that was no way for a man supposed to be deeply in love to behave. He hadn't even found time, apparently, to buy her a ring!

'I suggest you don't waste either your time or your money buying me an engagement ring,' she said coldly, 'since it strikes me that

111

we may not be as well suited as we thought. It won't do either of us any harm to think about it a bit longer before becoming engaged.'

She had Rudge's full attention now. He was staring at her with his brows drawn together in a frown of disbelief.

'You don't mean that, Sandie? You don't really mean you've changed your mind about marrying me? Why, that's ridiculous—absurd...'

'Is it? If we can't agree about fundamentals, Rudge, it's perhaps better that we don't get married. Even you must see that.'

'Of course we agree about fundamentals!' Rudge said angrily. 'Now who is making a mountain out of a molehill! Whether I can follow up my hunch or not can hardly be called a fundamental of life, can it?'

'I think it can!' Sandie said, tossing her head. 'I've no wish to marry a man who is going to forget I exist every time he thinks he's on to some wild, improbable story.'

'I haven't forgotten your existence, as you put it!' Rudge defended himself and at the same time, resented having to do so. 'We had dinner together last night and lunch today and damn it all, Sandie, I don't see why the hell I should defend my actions to you. I'll do as I think best, regardless of what you or Newman or any other damn person says. I wasn't sure half an hour ago what I'd do about the blasted story, but now I am sure. I'm not going to drop it, understand? First Newman threatens me with the sack. Then you threaten me with a broken engagement. Well, go ahead, if that's the way you want it. You accused me of not showing you enough love. Now I'm accusing you. If you break off our engagement, I'll know it's because you don't love me enough to back me up, right or wrong. So it's your decision now. Let me know when you've made up your mind.'

He pushed back his chair and beckoned the waiter for his bill. Sandie reached for her jacket and slowly put her arms into the sleeves. She was deeply upset, but determined not to let Rudge see it. Let him be the one to make up this quarrel for she would not. She wasn't dependent upon him and no matter how desperate she was to be back on the old loving terms with him once more, she was not going to allow him to ride roughshod over her pride.

Neither spoke whilst Rudge paid the bill and followed Sandie out to the car. In silence they got in and Rudge drove her back to the school. In silence she got out by the school gates. She was waiting for Rudge to speak but he did not do so until she was several yards away from the car. Then he called after her:

'Shall I pick you up here this evening?'

She felt a swift thrill of triumph. He did not really intend to make the break final. But instead of meeting him half way and accepting the hand stretched out for reconciliation, she

113

called back coolly:

'Just as you like. I may be late . . .'

Furiously, Rudge slammed the car into gear and turned out into the main road. For two pins he would have lifted Sandie up then and there in front of the school and spanked her. She deserved it. It hadn't been a bit easy for him to be the one to speak first, especially when he felt that she had been the cause of the quarrel, not himself. But he hated the idea of parting from her with this horrible coldness between them and he'd weakened at the last moment, making a last appeal. And that was her reaction . . . 'I may be late!'

'So you be late, my girl!' he thought. 'I'll give you exactly two minutes this evening and that's your lot—after that I'll be off and you can walk home!'

Little did Rudge think that it would be he who was late, not Sandie. And not just two minutes late but nearly two hours. By that time Sandie had long since given him up and walked home to cry her eyes out in the privacy of her locked flat.

NINE

Sandie did not cry for long. Her initial resentment at the way Rudge was treating her gave way to an angry determination not to let him 'push her around' a moment longer. As far as she was concerned, the engagement was off. She could do without him. All her adult life she had been independent and this, her first experience of love, was proving to her that she wasn't the type to become the adoring slave of any man. If Rudge couldn't treat her as an equal, then there was no hope for their marriage. She didn't want his love at the price of her own freedom—and that was what this stupid quarrel really boiled down to. He expected her to put her own life on one side and sit patiently on the perimeter of his, waiting until he should choose to notice her again.

Thoroughly depressed and with every moment that passed more and more resentful, Sandie made herself a snack and tried not to look at the clock on the mantel shelf ticking away the minutes. She was angry with herself because she knew that she was waiting either for Rudge's ring at the bell or for a telephone call from him. She wanted not to care whether she ever saw him again. It infuriated her that there was still an ungovernable part of her which persisted in wanting to be back on the old happy footing with Rudge. Her heart would not obey her mind.

She made coffee and taking the telephone off its rest, congratulated herself at finding this method of stopping herself waiting for Rudge to ring. If he came to the door she would not answer. Meanwhile, she had, she told herself, other more important things to think about—little Julia Forbes.

Mrs Sinclair had been very kind to the child but quite firm about Julia telling her parents the truth with no further delay. As Mrs Sinclair had explained to Sandie later, the school doctor had said this was not a matter he could deal with. Julia would have to go to her own family doctor, preferably with her parents. No matter how frightened the child was, Mr and Mrs Forbes ought to be told.

Julia, nearly hysterical, had said she would rather kill herself; that Mrs Sinclair could not know how angry her father would be. In the end, Mrs Sinclair had said she would take the child home after school and herself explain to the parents what it was feared had happened to their daughter. By now, the interview should be over and at least Julia would have this hurdle behind her. From now on, Sandie hoped, the girl would at least have her mother to advise and help her even if the father was 'difficult'. They could only hope that Julia's fears were finally proved wrong.

Sandie picked up some exercise books she had brought home to correct but could not concentrate upon them. The picture of Julia's pale, distraught little face kept impinging itself upon the page in front of her. It seemed terrible to Sandie that any child should be so afraid of her father's wrath. No matter what terrible thing she had done, surely she should be able to feel confident at least of her father's love and understanding. She wondered what would happen if the father were to turn Julia out of the house like a Victorian parent. It still happened these days. No doubt the Social Services would come to the rescue and poor Julia could probably have an abortion or she would be sent to a Mothers' and Babies' Home.

Mrs Sinclair had assured Sandie that if the doctor's report was in the affirmative, someone with experience of such disasters would be alerted to advise and guide them all.

Sandie drew a long sigh. The terrible effect on the girl's life at this stage of her development appalled her. Julia was one of her most promising pupils and a very nice girl. It was shocking to reflect that a careless moment of thoughtless, cruel selfishness on the part of that boy could have such frightful repercussions. It was little use people advocating sex instruction and birth control for teenagers as a solution to all the problems. Julia was not promiscuous and could not have known when she agreed to be driven home by the boy that he would behave in such an animal fashion. No doubt her parents had warned her such things could happen but the very young never took such warnings seriously. Julia would never have anticipated being forced against her will, accustomed as she was to going around with a boy like Tony

Dodd. He was a quiet, well-mannered decent boy—a bit of an idealist, a dreamer. He was at the opposite end of the pole to the degenerate young pop singer. Sandie did not like to think what this would do to Tony—and he must surely find out eventually. Julia had told her this morning after art class that she was finding it very difficult to keep Tony at bay. She had told him she didn't want to see or talk to him but he, understandably enough, refused to accept this extraordinary behaviour from Julia until he knew the reason why. Mistakenly, he believed the minor tiff they had had before the rock concert was the cause of it. Whatever he had said or done to upset her, he said, she must know he was sorry and forgive him. In tears Julia told Sandie that this was the worst part of all—Tony asking her forgiveness when it was all her fault.

Sandie had tried to offer what comfort she could. In the first place, Julia's fears could be unfounded—the pregnancy had not yet been confirmed. In the second place, it had not been her fault. Tony had known her for years and would realise that it wasn't her fault but that she had been the victim of Mike Shaw. He would not condemn her.

But nothing could console Julia. She never doubted that she was going to have a baby—she felt so sick in the morning and she was sure it wasn't nerves, for she felt hungry immediately afterwards! As to Tony, even if he believed she hadn't meant any of this to happen, he couldn't go on loving her. No one would ever love her now. She would never be able to get married. She wouldn't even be able to go on with her art studies and get to college. Everything was over, finished before it had scarcely begun. She wished over and over again that she were dead.

Although all Sandie's natural instincts prompted her to sympathise and comfort the girl, she somehow managed to speak sharply. She felt that she must get the idea out of Julia's mind that death was the answer. It was the coward's way out, she told Julia. She, Sandie, would lose any respect she had for a girl who took this easy and selfish way to escape consequences. Julia must never forget that any such action would hurt, even injure, others for the rest of their lives—her parents. Tony, even Sandie herself, for she would always feel she had failed to help and support one of her favourite pupils. There was a way out—she could legally get rid of the baby.

Julia had clung to her, sobbing uncontrollably. From the hysterical outpourings, Sandie understood two things— first that Julia thought abortion wicked—that nothing would ever make her murder her baby, for that was how she would feel if she had an abortion—a murderess; that no matter what happened, what hardships she had to endure, she'd never, never consent to such a wicked hateful idea.

Sandie, trying to soothe Julia's hysterics, also realised just how much her own affection for Julia and the child's for her counted at this time. She had not realised to what extent Julia had become dependent upon her. It seemed the girl did not get on too well with either her mother or her father. Sandie had come to symbolise for Julia the mother figure she craved—someone attractive, sharing her own interests in art, educated, intelligent and above all, sympathetic. Poor Mrs Forbes apparently lacked most of these essentials and although she obviously did love her daughter, she was so dominated by the father that she could never stand up to him and support Julia if it meant going against him.

Sandie realised that she was becoming, however involuntarily, very deeply involved with the girl. She knew that it was best to keep on less emotional levels with her pupils and even more important, never to come between a child and its parents. But Julia was building up the relationship because of her own desperate need for a mother figure. It was not Sandie wanting a doting, idolising daughter! Julia might think of her as old enough to be her mother, but Sandie knew it wasn't so long ago that she had been as young and vulnerable as Julia. She felt quite as young and vulnerable now and would very much have liked a mother of her own to guide and advise her how to behave with Rudge. Was she being unfair to him? Or he to her? Must marriage, a real marriage of the mind as well as the body, inevitably mean the denying of all self interest? And if so, what about Rudge doing some of the self denial?

Suddenly Sandie felt herself doubting whether or not she was really in love. Their relationship seemed to have changed subtly since she had permitted Rudge to make love to her. Was this where she had gone wrong? But she had wanted it as much as he had; she had found the experience rewarding and beautiful and exciting and if anything, loved him even more after than before. Or was it different for a man and, as she had so often read, he lost interest once he had 'conquered' the female.

As if in the direct denial of her fears, the front door bell rang. Sandie felt the blood rush to her cheeks. She covered her mouth with her hands, stifling the cry that nearly burst from her. She had no doubt it *was* Rudge.

He knocked. Rang again. Still she did not reply. Finally, he called out to her.

'Sandie, I know you're there. Please open the door!'

She got up and went to the door, telling herself that it was a sign of weakness to lock him out. If she didn't want to see him again, she had only to say so and he would go. Not to let him in was to show him that she was afraid of his physical hold over her . . .

She wrenched open the door and they stood looking at one another. Then Rudge took a step forward, kicked the door shut with his heel and pulled her roughly into his arms. At once she began to fight him, struggling to free herself from his embrace, but he held her firmly until she ceased resisting him. Then he kissed her.

For a moment he felt her body go slack and then move towards him in an unconscious response. He let go one of her hands so that he could encircle her waist but at once, she pulled her mouth away from his and slapped him hard across the cheek. Immediately, he released her and stood staring down at her hot, angry face, his cheek stinging from the blow she had just delivered.

'Mind telling me what that's for?' he asked coldly.

He expected a furious onslaught of words but to his surprise—the second within a minute—she burst into tears. This time she offered no resistance as he drew her gently back into his arms.

'I'm sorry!' she gulped. 'I didn't mean to hit you. I was so hurt, s-s-so angry. Oh, I hate you, Bob Rudgely. I *hate* you!'

'I know, sweetheart, and I hate you, too,' he said as he kissed her lips. They were salty from her tears. He wiped her cheeks gently.

She sniffed, blew into her handkerchief, rubbed her eyes and allowed him to pull her down on to the sofa. She was still angry with him, but at the same time, confusingly, she felt weak with relief at being back in his arms again.

'Now, let's have it all out!' Rudge said calmly as he nestled her head into his shoulder. 'It's because I was late again picking you up after school, I suppose. Well, at least give me a chance to explain, darling. I swear I didn't mean to be late—although I *was* annoyed at the way you behaved at lunchtime. I had every intention of meeting you on the dot but...'

'Don't tell me. I don't want to hear. You don't have to make excuses, I just thought...' She turned to look up at him, biting her lip and frowning in her effort to make him understand. 'I began to wonder if we really ought to get married, Rudge, I mean, if we really are suited to each other. I've been my own master for years and I'm not sure I'd be any good as a wife. I...'

Rudge interrupted her with a long, searching kiss.

'You'll make a perfect wife!' he whispered, his hands reaching beneath her sweater to touch the warm, soft, bare flesh. 'I love you, Sandie.'

But she drew away from him, her eyes uneasy.

'What we feel now . . .' she said hesitantly . . . 'it isn't *love,* Rudge.'

'I love you—and I want you!' Rudge said, his lips against her neck. 'Isn't that enough? What's wrong with wanting each other?'

'Nothing, nothing!' she cried. 'But sex doesn't solve anything. It only seems to complicate things. Oh, Rudge, try to understand. I do want you . . . I'd like to make love now, only . . .'

He drew away and stared down at her, his own eyes puzzled.

'You mean you don't believe I really do love you?'

Sandie drew a deep sigh.

'In a way I suppose I do mean that. I'm not even sure if I love you. Before you came, I'd made up my mind I wouldn't see you—not if you rang and knocked at the door all night. I . . . Rudge, I'm sorry if I'm not making much sense. I'm not sure if I understand myself.'

'Something must have happened to make you change your mind so suddenly. I can't believe this is all because I was late for our rendezvous. That would be too trivial . . . and I can explain. There *was* a reason though I don't think it should be necessary for me to give it. You have to trust me, Sandie. Trust my love for you too. What has happened to make you doubt me?'

Sandie remained silent. Now that Rudge had pointed out how trivial his 'offence' really

124

was, she couldn't tell him that this had been the root cause of the trouble. She wasn't even sure it was so simple. It could have something to do with Julia . . . with her own feeling of revulsion for the way that boy had raped her with complete disregard for anything but his own beastly desires. Without quite realising it, she had aligned herself on Julia's—the feminine side—against male selfishness and lust. Sex, even though it was important to a woman, wasn't *all* important. Love was an essential in Sandie's view. And if Rudge couldn't love her, then she didn't want him to make love to her, no matter how much her body betrayed her into a physical longing to give herself to him again and again.

He watched the changing expressions of her face and said shrewdly:

'If you want me to understand, you must share your thoughts, darling. Tell me—what's upset you?'

She told him briefly about her fears for Julia—her feelings when the child had broken down and clung to her.

'I know she isn't my child, Rudge, but I almost felt as if she were my responsibility somehow. I'm worried for her; upset for her. I suppose subconsciously I've been personally affected by what has been done to her. I don't mean I am afraid of you . . . but I think I am a little afraid suddenly of sex. I don't know . . . until you showed me . . . what a powerful and strong emotion it was. I always believed that an intelligent, balanced person could keep complete control over their physical appetites. But . . .'

'You've changed your mind?' Rudge asked gently as she hesitated.

'Yes! I found myself wanting you to make love to me just now even though I hated you.'

'Or thought you hated me?' Rudge suggested. 'You were cross and upset and emotionally overwrought and wanted to hate me. But maybe in this instance, Sandie, your heart is being wiser than your head. I think you know very well, deep down, how much I love you; that you still love me. I think all this bother with Julia has made you unusually strung-up and tense and sensitive and I picked this unfortunate moment to, so you think, let you down. Darling, we must keep a clear perspective about all this. We won't make love if you don't want to. I accept that. But I can't sit here and listen to you doubting my love for you. I have no doubts at all. Why should you?'

'Oh, Rudge!' Her arms went round him almost involuntarily. She had forgotten until this moment just how much she did love him. He pulled her closer to him.

'I love you, Sandie—every little independent inch of you. I love you when you're cross and even when you swiped me just now.'

'Darling, I'm sorry. I'm so sorry!' she

capitulated instantly, urgently. 'I don't know what made me do it. I've never done such a thing to anyone in my life before. It was unforgivable.'

To her surprise she saw Rudge smiling.

'I forgive the unforgivable. It proves you *care*!' he said wisely. 'You were hurt by what you thought my neglect and you wanted to hurt back. You did, too!' he added grinning.

She reached up and kissed his cheek where it was still faintly red from her handprint. She touched it with her fingertip regretfully but he caught her hand and pressed it to his lips. A moment later, she was helpless in his arms. The last time, he had been gentle, tender, infinitely patient in his love-making. This time it was all quite different. He possessed her fiercely, hungrily and quickly and Sandie found her own responses matching his. Amidst all the disconnected, incoherent thoughts that chased through her mind she knew an extraordinary surprise that it could be like this—such a deep strong urgency that swept away all barriers. Their quarrels, her own uncertainties were dwarfed into insignificance beneath the violence of their loving.

'You do still love me!' Rudge said triumphantly when it was over. 'Or it couldn't have been like that.'

She nodded speechlessly. That was the way she felt. Now, at this moment, she was no longer unsure about the rightness of their getting married. She wanted to marry Rudge soon—as soon as possible. She wanted never to be separated from him again. She wanted . . .

'I wish we were married—*now!*' Rudge broke in on her thoughts as if he shared them as they had shared their loving.

'Soon!' Sandie whispered. 'We'll fix a date soon, darling.'

In a little while she went to the kitchen and cooked him a meal. They had coffee afterwards and Rudge said regretfully that he ought to go.

'Someone has to look after your reputation,' he said. 'It's midnight, darling, and your neighbours will be aghast to see me leaving your flat in the dead of night. I wish I could stay all night. I want to sleep with you— not the way that sounds, but really sleep with you all night long with my arms around you.'

'Rudge, you never did explain why you were delayed,' she said after he had kissed her good night.

'Another time, darling. If I don't go this minute, I shall never go. I don't seem able to have enough of you. I . . .'

He broke off to kiss her yet again and she pressed closer to him, her own need growing to match his.

'Make me leave now!' he begged, but she could not. She made no effort to stop him as he began slowly to undress her. Instead, she unbuttoned his shirt and slipped her arms through the opening so that she could feel his strong muscular back with her hands. Her clothes fell to the floor and he lifted her with ease, as if she were a child, and carried her to the divan. She lay with her eyes closed while he undressed and opened them as he came towards her like a young Adonis.

'I never realised men could be beautiful!' she said as she held out her arms to him.

It was only later, after Rudge had finally left her, that she thought of all that had happened and realised with dismay that it could never be like that for poor little Julia. No matter what happened in the future, when eventually she did fall in love, the thought of that first ugly experience could never be totally erased from her mind.

As she climbed into a hot bath and lay there tired but filled with contentment, Sandie's happiness was clouded by a tinge of guilt that she should have so much when another human being was wishing she was dead.

TEN

Sandra eyed the trumpeting, scarlet-faced individual confronting her with mounting anger. She had accepted without hesitation Mrs Sinclair's request to her to visit Julia's parents. It seemed that Mrs Sinclair herself had been singularly unsuccessful in handling the whole affair.

'I must have antagonised Mr Forbes somehow!' she had confessed to the young art teacher. Far from enlisting his sympathetic understanding and support of his daughter, I seem to have aroused the very worst possible reaction—you know, Sandra—the "never darken my door again, you are no child of mine" kind of remark. With Julia in tears and Mrs Forbes obviously unwilling to come out on either side, I felt I was getting nowhere. Will you go and see them, Sandra? Julia is fond of you and perhaps Mr Forbes won't be so uncooperative with a pretty young girl as he was with an elderly headmistress!'

Mrs Sinclair had an interview with the local social worker before going to visit the Forbes. There would be a further interview when Sandie had to report her own success or failure to get Julia's parents to take at least a sympathetic attitude towards their child's predicament.

'Look, Mr Forbes, before you condemn Julia further, may I remind you that none of this was her fault?' Sandra said now. 'That perhaps the very innocence you are so concerned about was the initial cause of all the trouble? If Julia were really the kind of girl you have just suggested, she would have known better than to allow that boy to take advantage of her.'

The rotund, perspiring angry father made an unsuccessful attempt to curb his irrational fury. What he could not stand was the *disgrace* this would bring upon his name, his family. He had understood from Mrs Sinclair that if rape could be proved the police would insist upon prosecuting the boy responsible. It was up to the Chief Constable to decide and neither Mrs Sinclair herself, nor the social worker and certainly not Julia, had any say in the matter although naturally what was best for Julia would be uppermost in everyone's mind.

It was not uppermost in Mr Forbes' mind. His own carefully guarded, long-worked-for good name was in jeopardy through no fault of his own and he wasn't going to accept the situation if he could help it. Julia would have to go—it didn't matter where so long as she was not under his roof, for all the neighbours to point a finger at. Just to think of what his customers would say was enough to send him into fresh panic.

'I bloody well don't give a damn *whose* fault it was!' he shouted at Sandie. 'I'm not keeping her and her brat here and that's flat.'

'Perhaps Mrs Forbes might disagree . . .' Sandie began when she was shouted down.

'My wife will do as I say. If I say Julia goes, she goes, so you can get that straight for a start.'

Sandie was forced to admit that there was

little hope of Julia's mother standing by her. All she could say was that she felt Julia should get rid of the baby but the girl stubbornly refused to accept this way out. As tall and thin as her husband was short and fat, the woman was obviously completely dominated by the bumptious, self-opinionated little man who faced her. Mrs Forbes was every bit as frightened of him as Julia was. Sandie wasn't in the least frightened for she knew the type— there were plenty in the school amongst the less intelligent of her boy pupils; those who had to resort to bullying and shouting to make a big show of strength they did not in fact possess. She knew Mr Forbes for exactly what he was—a frightened little man who was up against something beyond his power to control.

But knowing him would not help to change him. She had tried unsuccessfully to plead with him to stand by Julia; she had tried reasoning. Now she tried for the last time to fight him with his own weapon—fear.

'Doesn't it worry you to think what people will say about you—throwing your fifteen-year-old daughter out of your house like some old-fashioned Victorian parent? People will talk, Mr Forbes, and in my opinion they'll condemn you for such behaviour to a child in this day and age.'

For a moment, the man seemed to hesitate as he considered Sandie's warning. She could almost see in that rather stupid red and aggressive face the effort it was costing him to have to weigh up the pros and cons. Through his eyes, she could see him trying to imagine a Julia, large with her pregnancy, walking along the street or into his shop for all to see her shame. No, he couldn't tolerate it. Right was right and wrong was wrong. Julia had done wrong—a shameful terrible thing. He'd campaigned against the abortion bill but now, just as furiously, he wished to God he hadn't. Getting rid of her child was the only way out—the *only* way to hush everything up. But there did not seem any likelihood of that; he'd rung up the doctor after the wretched girl had returned with her mother with the terrible news confirmed and told him flatly to get rid of the baby. All he had had in reply was a cool: 'The baby will be born early next year, Mr Forbes. Julia feels very strongly against abortion and I would not consider operating against her will. There is no reason why she and the baby shouldn't be perfectly healthy. Your wife will be in touch with the social worker who will give you all the advice you need.'

So that was that. At first he'd felt stunned— too horrified to make himself believe that this could have happened to *his* daughter. When he knew there was no hope it was all a mistake, he gave way to a violent anger which, even now, face to face with this slip of a girl who was supposed to be Julia's teacher, he could barely control.

'As far as I am concerned,' he told Sandie now, 'Julia is no longer my daughter. The sooner she leaves the house the better pleased I'll be. I've always said there wasn't enough discipline in schools today. You teachers are far too permissive. Well, let's see how you and your social services get the girl out of this mess because I don't intend to get involved and that's my final word.'

Sandie made a last effort at reason.

'You are involved, whether you wish it or not, Mr Forbes. You might turn Julia out of her home but you are still her legal guardian and it is you who will have to be approached for any decisions as to Julia's welfare. I do beg of you, as her father, to try to see this from her point of view. Naturally she is frightened, ashamed— about as insecure as any young girl could be, faced with this kind of a problem. The support of her family, of you, her father, could make all the difference to her. You should be proud that she has the courage and will to resist abortion no matter how much simpler this would make things for her. She . . .'

'I won't hear another word!' Mr Forbes interrupted, jumping to his feet and flinging open the door. 'Will you kindly leave my house and tell that headmistress I don't wish to see her here again either. Good day, Miss White.'

Sandie had no alternative but to go. She seemed to be making matters worse for Julia rather than better. She wondered where the child was, for the house had been silent when Mr Forbes had opened the door to her. Mrs Forbes had remained only for a moment before hurriedly leaving the room when her husband started to lose his temper.

Sandie was more than a little depressed as she walked back up the High Street towards her flat. Mrs Sinclair would be most disappointed to hear of her failure to change Mr Forbes' attitude. Perhaps given a few weeks to get over the initial shock, he would come round to a less selfish point of view. In the meanwhile, what kind of home life would that poor child have?

Perhaps she was not altogether surprised to find Julia sitting on the top landing outside her own front door, looking like a forlorn lost puppy. She jumped up as Sandie approached and flung herself at her young teacher, her face red and blotchy with tears.

'I've run away!' she gasped. 'You've got to help me. Oh, please, Miss White, help me . . .'

Sandie disentangled the sobbing child and unlocking her door, led her into the flat and settled her down in an armchair. Then she made a cup of tea which she forced Julia to drink before she would discuss anything with her. The girl was much calmer when eventually Sandie sat down opposite her and said gently:

'I suppose you didn't tell your parents you intended to come here, did you?'

Julia shook her head, the dark hair falling across her damp cheeks.

'Then I shall have to tell them . . .' Sandie began but Julia broke in bitterly:

'They won't care. They'll be glad I've gone. I heard what Dad said to you; I was upstairs listening all the time. He hates me—he'd be glad if I died. Last night he said . . .' her voice faltered on a broken little sob . . . 'he said I should get rid of the baby! But I couldn't, Miss White, I couldn't. It's my baby. I don't want it killed.' She ended in a fresh flood of tears.

'Oh, Julia!' Sandie whispered, horrified and filled with compassion. 'Of course not—no one can make you have an abortion if you don't want it. I'm sure your father only suggested it because he felt it would make things so much easier for you.'

'Let me stay with you!' Julia cried suddenly, her fingers digging into Sandie's arms in panicky desperation. 'I promise I won't be a nuisance. I'll clean the place for you and do the cooking and washing and everything. I won't be any trouble. Please, Miss White, *please.*'

Sandie realised the girl was near to hysteria . . . and small wonder, she thought bitterly, if she had overheard the conversation between her father and herself. Of course she couldn't keep Julia here. It was out of the question . . . her family wouldn't agree even if she, herself, were prepared to sacrifice her own privacy. Now that she and Rudge . . .

Sandie's thoughts came to an abrupt halt at this point. She continued rocking Julia in her arms, murmuring soothing words and stroking the child's hair while her mind began to race in a different direction. With Julia living here with her, she and Rudge would be unable to give way to the violent temptations that had twice swept them off their feet. They would be forced to control their feelings and no matter how much she, Sandie, might regret this later, it suddenly seemed an extremely sensible, logical step to take. She did not believe in sex outside marriage. If true love existed, then marriage was the answer. If it did not, sex only complicated matters. Besides which, how could she, a teacher, face the young girls in her charge knowing that she was too weak, herself, to practise the moral behaviour she preached to them?

Not only was there this personal reason for agreeing to Julia's living here with her, but there was also her own strong desire to help the child in any way she could. She was too kind, too soft-hearted, to be able to stand by in silence whilst a young girl like Julia was in need of her help and understanding.

'Julia, I can't promise anything,' she said cautiously, 'because I don't know if it is

137

possible for you to live here with me. I am not one of your relatives—nor even a friend of your parents. Your father and mother would have to approve of such an arrangement. Then, too, the social worker may say it isn't permissible. I just don't know what the law is in a case like yours.'

'But you'd let me come—if it is allowed?' The girl's eyes still brimming with tears, bored into Sandie's, filled with hope, appeal, a desperate wish to believe. If Sandie was beginning to feel any regret at her hasty decision, it was swept to one side when she saw what this straw meant to the girl.

'*If* it can be arranged!' she said. 'But you mustn't count on it yet, Julia. At any rate, you shall stay here tonight. I'll drop a note in at your home to let your parents know you are here. We don't want to start off on the wrong foot by letting them think I've kidnapped you, do we?'

It was more than Julia could do to manage a smile but she nodded her head, the dark hair cascading over her face sticking to the wet patches on her cheeks left by her tears.

'I think I'd better let Mrs Sinclair know, too,' Sandie said, as much to herself as to Julia. 'She may wish to advise the social worker. Now, Julia, into bed. You look half dead. I'm going to make you a hot drink and give you two aspirins and you're to go to sleep. You'll feel quite different in the morning, you see. I'm going to make up the divan in the boxroom for you. It's small, I know, but you'll be quite cosy and comfortable in there. You go and wash your face and I'll find one of my nighties for you.'

She was strangely touched by Julia's feminine yet childish pleasure when she lent her one of her prettiest frilly nylon shorty nighties. Julia held it up against her with a gasp.

'Can I really borrow it? I'll be ever so careful!' she promised and for the first time, she smiled. 'My Mum wouldn't half create if she could see me wearing a see-through! She still makes me wear wincyette pyjamas. Once I saved up and bought a nightie a bit like this at Dorothy Perkins but when Mum saw it, she made me burn it.'

Silently, Sandie sighed. No wonder this child's life was in such a mess. It was asking for trouble in this day and age for a parent to harp on Victorian standards of upbringing. Sooner or later children had to face the real world. Surely it was far better to face it simply and naturally, knowing what life was about. If Julia had come from a different background, she might not be in this mess now.

But half an hour later, as she walked down the road to the nearest phone box to telephone Mrs Sinclair and Rudge out of Julia's hearing, Sandie began to regret her impulsive half promise. She could, of course, get out of it on the grounds that she had not guaranteed to offer Julia a home but she doubted if her conscience would permit this easy way out. When she'd tucked Julia into bed and told her she would be going out for a while, the girl had clung to her like a small bewildered child. Already Julia was depending upon her to stand by her; and by her emotional dependence, Julia had made Sandie morally responsible for her future well-being.

Mrs Sinclair was cautious in giving her approval.

'I suppose you do realise what you are undertaking? Abandoned by her own parents, the child will naturally turn to you, Sandra. Do you really want to take this on? There is absolutely no obligation upon you to do so, you know.'

'Yes, I know! But I feel I should do anything I can to help. Perhaps it's because I've been on my own and I know how lonely it can be. Call my motives humanitarian, if you like, but I don't think I could just opt out— pretend to myself that Julia's future was no concern of mine. If she were to do anything desperate, I'd *feel* responsible for having failed to help when I could.'

'It's very nice of you, Sandra, although I don't know if I should encourage you. I suppose we'll have to leave the ultimate decision to the social worker and to Julia's parents. *They* might not approve. I'm sorry you had such a bad time with the father; a hopeless case, I'm afraid. Her mother might have stood by her if she weren't so totally dominated by her husband.'

If Mrs Sinclair's opinion was hardly reassuring, Rudge's comments were flatly disapproving.

'You must be out of your mind, Sandie. What can have possessed you to become involved in such a way? Helping the child is one thing; reorganising your whole life for her is another. You must rescind the offer at once—say you've considered all the implications and changed your mind.'

As Rudge spoke, Sandie felt the wavering core of uncertainty suddenly harden into resolve to go through with it. It was not for Rudge to decide what she should and should not do. He was being utterly selfish—seeing everything only from his own point of view. She told him so and his voice came back over the line angry and accusing.

'If you really want to know the truth, Sandie, I hadn't until this very moment considered how it would affect *me*. I was thinking only of you. But now that you've brought it up, what about us? I'm not taking on responsibility for a pregnant schoolgirl just because the girl I'm engaged to is her teacher!'

'We're *not* engaged!' Sandie flared back. 'And what I do with my life is my business.'

'Good God, Sandie, have you gone out of your mind? What in heaven's name is wrong with you all of a sudden? When we parted we were on the very best terms. Why this now? Just because I disapprove of you becoming involved in a matter where you have no obligations, moral or otherwise? Can't you see I'm just trying to protect *you*—'

Because she realised that Rudge could very well be right; because she herself was so uncertain that her decision was for the best, Sandie felt her resolve weaken. Rudge, sensing her hesitation, added swiftly:

'I want to marry you, Sandie, and you said you wanted to marry me. If you're going to make yourself responsible for Julia for the next nine months, how can we possibly get married? If you persist in this stupid idea, I shall begin to think you are deliberately trying to put a barrier in the way of our marriage.'

Sandie drew in her breath sharply. Rudge's words struck an answering chord in her heart. She hadn't been sure about wanting to marry him; sure that she wanted him physically, yes, but to tie herself down permanently in marriage? No, she wasn't sure and he could very well be right—Julia would make a very solid barrier against marriage to Rudge. If she undertook to look after Julia at least until the girl went to a Mothers' and Babies' Home, she would have to put her personal life on one side. It would give her a breathing space . . .

time to think; to sort out how she really felt about Rudge, about her own feelings.

'We don't *have* to get married at once,' she said in a small quiet voice. 'If you really do love me, Rudge, you'll wait those few months. If you can't—or won't—then it means you don't really love me at all.'

There was a moment's uneasy silence before Rudge burst out:

'You talk of love and yet you're preparing to put me second to a girl who means nothing at all to you? Don't lecture me about love, Sandie, if that's the way you feel!'

It should have ended there—the whole sudden stupid argument. Rudge was, of course, quite right. She *should* put him first. But she couldn't bring herself to admit it. The fact was, she was uncertain of *herself*, not of him. She couldn't be sure she really loved him although deep down inside, she did believe he loved her. She just wasn't ready to give up her independence.

On the other hand, Rudge was being totally selfish, she told herself. Everyone had certain obligations to society. Someone had to care for girls like Julia. If everyone took the easy, selfish way out, what kind of a world were the Julias of this life growing up to find? Rejected by parents, by society, small wonder if they developed into hard, bitter, cynical adults. With a little kindness, a little love and understanding now, Julia could yet become a useful member of society. If everyone put self first, as Rudge suggested, what kind of an example were they setting the young?

'I've never heard such a load of rubbish!' Rudge said unguardedly when Sandie tried to explain her point of view. In fact, she had touched his conscience a little, made him realise that he really *didn't* care what happened to Julia. The only thing that mattered right now was Sandie and his personal relationship with her. So he was selfish. But Sandie was being ridiculously the opposite. There was just no need to sacrifice herself and him. There was a perfectly good Welfare State to look after the girl. Her parents were ultimately responsible. Why should Sandie, only a girl herself, take on obligations that were most certainly not hers?

'I'm sorry you feel that way, Rudge. Everything you say only makes me more certain not to rush into marriage. We don't after all see life the same way, do we?'

'That's silly. Of course I realise people have social responsibilities to each other. But there are limits, Sandie. Look, darling, don't please say any more now. I'm coming round to see you this evening . . .' He broke off, realising that with Julia in the flat, any kind of personal conversation would be impossible. He felt cheated, angry and desperate all at once. 'I'll pick you up at your flat in an hour's time,' he said. 'We'll go for a run in the car and talk this whole thing out. Okay?'

It ought to have been but Sandie was afraid Rudge might very well talk her round to his point of view. She didn't want to be made to change her mind by Rudge or anyone else. She was sufficiently adult and responsible to decide for herself what she should or should not do.

'There really isn't any point discussing things at this stage, Rudge,' she said stiffly. 'I don't even know yet if Julia would be allowed to stay with me. Give me a ring tomorrow and we'll talk about it then.'

Furious, hurt and failing completely to understand what had got into Sandie, Rudge put down the receiver. Silently, but without any real conviction, he told himself that if this was an example of the way Sandie loved him, he was lucky to be discovering it now, before he had committed himself irrevocably to marriage. This certainly wasn't his idea of how an engaged couple behaved.

He took himself off to The Waterman's Arms with the idea of getting slowly and solitarily drunk.

ELEVEN

In the Club House, Cilla Newman was also having a great deal too much to drink. The week had come full circle. She was due at

Philip Hurst's house but for the first time in her life, she had made up her mind to defy him—on account of Bill.

When she had turned up at tea-time for her golf lesson, she had every intention of keeping her appointment with Philip afterwards. Fear of the consequences if she did not do so outweighed her repugnance for the man. But during her lesson Bill had been unusually charming and attentive.

At first she had not fully understood why. Until today, he had resisted all her efforts to attract him. By the time they reached the sixteenth hole, Bill suddenly and unexpectedly confided in her that he was, as he put it, nursing a broken heart. It seemed that he had learned from Bob Rudgely over lunch that he was engaged to Sandra White and Bill had had reluctantly to accept that his chances with Sandra were at an end.

'Frankly, I was more than half way in love with her,' Bill told Cilla, surprising himself as much as his companion with his confidences. 'Oh, well, I suppose I should accept that the best man has won. But I had hoped, as they seemed to quarrel quite a bit, that the friendship would break up and I'd get a look in.'

Tactfully Cilla avoided the pitfall of telling Bill he was well rid of Sandie. Instead, she offered condolences and suggested that there were other women in the world and several she could name who found Bill very attractive indeed.

'I expect there have been occasions when I've shocked you a little by letting you know I find you attractive, too!' she had concluded in a casual semi-humorous tone that meant he was not to think she was talking too seriously.

Bill's reactions had been copy-book. With his pride smarting from Sandie's indifference to him, he was receptive to any kind of compliment and Cilla Newman's compliments were both welcome and soothing if not exactly exciting. She knew how to flatter a man and he was male enough to fall for flattery no matter from whom it came.

It was he who suggested a drink when the lesson ended and Cilla, telling herself that she still had plenty of time to go to Philip's later, readily agreed.

But they had both drunk steadily and systematically for the past two hours and Bill, not having Cilla's capacity for hard drinking, was no longer responsible for his actions. He fell in readily with Cilla's suggestion to repair to The Waterman's Arms to continue their drinking session away from the constant interruptions of other Club members who were not quite on the same level of insobriety as they were.

'S'long as you drive, Cilla!' he said. 'Doubt I'd pash the breathlysher tesht!'

The combination of fresh air as they walked

out to the car park and the simultaneous striking of eight o'clock by the village church bell, caused Cilla to pause for a moment as she fitted the key into the ignition. She ought to put in an appearance at dinner or Gerald would start asking awkward questions—not that he cared personally what she was up to but he expected her to keep up appearances of being a happily married couple in front of the two servants they employed. Then there was Philip. Would he *dare* make trouble? If he did . . .

But she put the thought quickly aside. She could go and see Philip tomorrow, tell him some story about a political meeting of Gerald's she'd had to attend. Meanwhile, Bill was slouched half asleep in the seat beside her and his hand lay innocently but still suggestively along her left leg. She studied him for a moment thoughtfully. A bit more to drink and he might pass out. But if he sobered up would he still want her?

'Are you hungry, Bill?' she asked. 'I am. I've got an idea. Let's buy a bottle or two and some sandwiches at the pub and go back to your place.'

Bill had a small cottage where he lived alone on the far perimeter of the golf course. They would have complete privacy there. In his present mood she would have no difficulty in seducing him.

Bill, himself, was conscious of very little. It

was important to him with his job to keep fit and he seldom drank anything but beer. Now the whisky fumes were swirling round his head and he realised vaguely that he was hopelessly tight. He was aware of Cilla's perfume as she bent over him; aware of the silky feel of her knee beneath his hand. At this moment she was nothing more to him than female, and therefore desirable. From time to time he thought he might enjoy making love to this woman. She wasn't Sandie but she was soft, silky, warm and apparently, willing.

He tried ineffectually to recall what it was about the woman beside him that he did not like. He couldn't remember. He recalled she was a good golfer, but this wasn't exactly the sort of fact he was searching for. The puzzle kept his confused thoughts well occupied whilst Cilla drove down to The Waterman's Arms. There, he staggered out obedient to Cilla's instructions and clutching the pound notes she thrust into his hands, pushed his way into the bar to buy a bottle of whisky and some sandwiches.

Whilst waiting to be served his eye was caught by a solitary drinker at the far end of the bar—Bob Rudgely. Bill stared at him with drunken intensity. He hated that man, though he couldn't precisely remember why— something to do with Sandie. Rudge caught his eye and lifted a hand in greeting but Bill ignored him. He wasn't going to be friendly with the chap who'd pinched the girl he wanted. For two pins or a pint, he'd knock him down; he'd . . .

'That'll be seven pounds, sir,' the barman interrupted his rising aggression. Bill promptly forgot Rudge and handing over the money, weaved his way out of the pub.

Rudge watched him go, still sober enough himself to realise that Bill was pretty drunk. He hoped he wasn't driving in that condition. The man wasn't fit to walk on his own, let alone drive.

With a sigh, Rudge stood up and followed Bill out into the car park. He stood for a moment trying to accustom his eyes to the sudden dark, searching for Bill's little red Mini. He couldn't see it or Bill. Then a car engine started and turning his head, Rudge caught sight of the Newmans' Jaguar, Cilla at the wheel. The car reversed and came towards him. As it passed, Rudge saw Bill slumped in the passenger seat. If Cilla recognised him, she gave no sign but accelerated sharply and swung out of the car park on to the road.

Rudge stood for a moment staring after the diminishing red lights of the Jag. Cilla Newman with Bill Wells? What would Sandie say to that, if she knew? So much for her high opinion of Wells.

Then he shrugged his shoulders and went back into the pub. It was no business of his what Wells or Cilla Newman did with their spare time. And it didn't look as if Sandie was going to be any of his business, either—not the way things were happening between them. He didn't understand women, full stop.

Depressed, morose and thoroughly disgruntled, Rudge ordered himself another pint and decided that he didn't much care if he never saw Sandie or Ashwyck again. If it wasn't for the story—that nagging, prickling feeling of being on to something big—he'd light out tonight and turn his back on the lot of them. Nothing was good here except the beer, he told himself with a sudden grin. Ashwyck might have the outward appearance of a sleepy, charmingly innocent English village but when you began to lift a few stones, it wasn't after all so sleepy, charming and innocent as it might seem to the casual observer. It was like a woman, he thought bitterly, made up to look the kind of person a man could be at peace with but under the make-up, hard, cruel, corrupt. Like Cilla Newman . . . yes, and possibly like Sandie, too. Who would have thought she could have been so hard, so unfeeling, so unloving . . .

He was back with his former feelings of bewilderment and resentment and neither left him during the remainder of the evening. They stayed with him until at closing time he went up to his room. There, an excess of self-pity combined with The Waterman's excellent beer helped him to fall quickly into a dreamless sleep.

*   *   *

Rudge parked his car on the road beside Baker's Pool and made his way dispiritedly along the footpath towards Philip Hurst's cottage. A slight hangover was increasing his sense of depression. The last time he'd been here was with Sandie. He didn't want to think about her and it irritated him that no matter what he was doing she kept nagging at his thoughts.

She had even managed to put a damper on his former enthusiasm to chase up the Mystery Man, he told himself ruefully as he squelched along the muddy path beneath murky dripping trees that were, in themselves, enough to depress anyone. He'd woken up this morning determined to pursue his story despite Frank Newman's discouragement, despite Sandie, despite his feelings that after all, it was a bit pointless. He was being driven by his own stubborn refusal to give up although at this precise moment, the slightest pretext could have swerved him from his purpose.

A long thick trailing bramble wound itself round his trouser leg and he was forced to pause to disentangle himself, pricking his finger in the process. A moment later a rotten branch which he was using as a stepping stone

152

across a particularly nasty puddle, snapped in half, splashing a stagnant muddy liquid over his shoes and socks. He swore softly and decided to stop for a moment and cool his temper with a quiet smoke.

He was lighting a cigarette when he heard a faint noise back along the path he had just travelled. Surprised to hear anyone about—it was not yet ten-thirty and surely Hurst would not have been to the village and back so early?—Rudge stood waiting beneath the dripping beech tree, peering through the damp mist to see who was coming.

Rudge saw and recognised Cilla Newman a full minute before she raised her bent head and paused to look around her nervously, as if sensing someone's presence. By this time he had slipped behind the tree which sheltered him. Only the sound of a twig snapping beneath his feet had warned her that someone other than herself might be about.

Rudge held his breath. He dared not peer around the tree so he could no longer see what she was doing. He hoped fervently that she wouldn't find him. He could offer no reason for concealing himself in the way he had instinctively done and he would look and feel extremely foolish if he were caught. But suddenly he heard her move forward again. Holding his breath, he slid further round the tree so that he would remain out of sight should she take a last look behind her.

A few minutes later she disappeared round a bend in the path; Rudge let his breath go and stepped out of hiding. Now his hangover, his feeling of depression and pointlessness had all gone. His senses were strung tight and his thoughts swirled. Cilla Newman—on her way to Philip Hurst's cottage! Nothing would make him believe she was on her way to buy another picture. There was some association between those two—there *had* to be—and he intended to find out what it was.

As Rudge followed cautiously behind Cilla, moving as silently as he could and keeping well to the edge of the path by the trees, he felt a moment's dislike of the role of spy he had allotted himself. He had never enjoyed the side of reporting that involved his prying into people's private lives. If it were simply a question of Cilla's having an affair with Hurst, then he'd keep their sordid little secret for what it was worth. Neither they nor anyone else would know he knew. But he had to find out if it was *only* an affair between the two. The accident at Baker's Pool had produced only two possible clues—and those so vague as to be almost meaningless—Philip Hurst's proximity to the scene of the accident—indeed the only person living within miles of it—and Cilla Newman's curious visit to Hurst's cottage in the ensuing week. Had there been any other clues of any kind, no one would have attached the slightest importance to either fact. Even without any other clues, no one but Rudge himself seemed to have felt there was the slightest suspicion attached to either Hurst or Cilla. Even he had been forced to accept that it was highly improbable either were involved.

But Cilla's presence here today altered everything. It was a dank cold unpleasant morning; no one in their right senses would be out in this wood for a walk, not even with a dog. It wasn't as if she were a friend of Hurst's—as far as Rudge knew Hurst had no friends, and Cilla herself had denied any kind of association with the man apart from that one visit to his studio to look at his paintings.

Rudge came to an abrupt halt as the cottage came into sight. Cilla was just disappearing through the door and Rudge realised that he had been a fraction of a second too late to see whether she had walked right in or had had to knock and be let in as would have happened if Hurst were not expecting her.

He paused uncertainly. He must know what was being said yet he was taking a severe risk of being heard if he approached too close to the cottage. He glanced round and observed an overgrown rhododendron bush spreading its thick glistening leaves in heavy drapes towards a half open window. If he could reach the shrub undetected, he could conceal himself there more than adequately.

Skirting the overgrown, weed-ridden garden in a wide circle, Rudge managed to reach his chosen hiding place. He could not have selected a better vantage point. Cilla Newman and Philip Hurst stood facing each other inside the window.

'I know I should have come yesterday, Philip, but at least try and be reasonable . . .' Cilla's voice sounded high-pitched, nervous and at the same time, angry and resentful. 'I told you it wasn't my fault. Gerald had a political meeting—or at least, he had to appear at a gathering, mainly women, and insisted I be there for appearances' sake. I didn't have any excuse *not* to go along. You must appreciate I can't control occasions like that.'

The man's reply was too low for Rudge to catch the meaning. But already he had heard enough to feel his eavesdropping vindicated. Cilla had betrayed the fact that she did know Hurst—very well, by the sound of it. Her self-admitted arrangement to meet him yesterday confirmed that this was no casual dropping-in. Moreover, she was lying. She had certainly not been at any political meeting with her husband.

'. . . please, Philip!' she was actually pleading now, her tone almost desperate. 'It's easy for you living here alone . . . you don't have to account for your actions. I do and Gerald's getting more and more difficult. We

156

had a violent scene this morning at breakfast and . . .'

'I'm not in the least interested in your sordid little domestic squabbles!' Now Rudge could hear every word as the man's voice raised its pitch in anger. 'Gerald . . .' the way he spoke the name was filled with scorn and derision . . . 'Gerald is hardly in a position to complain, is he? Don't try and make out he told you not to come here any more, I'm not such a fool as to believe your husband values your faithfulness more than his career.'

'You're a filthy, rotten no-good . . .'

Her words halted abruptly as the clear sharp sound of a slap followed by a muffled cry reached Rudge's ears. Instinctively he half rose from his crouched position, his first thought to protect the woman if there was to be physical violence, but he was quickly halted by the sound of a laugh from Philip Hurst and his voice saying:

'Don't try to pretend with me, my dear. I know you. You made it quite clear last week that you wanted to put an end to our interesting little affair but I thought I made it equally clear that I had no intention of letting you do so.'

Cilla's reply came in a low, helpless voice. 'I can't see how you can get any pleasure out of it, Philip, knowing it's against my will.'

Philip laughed.

'Then   you   are   losing   your   usual

157

perceptiveness, my dear Cilla. Quite frankly—
and we are being frank, aren't we . . . ?'—the
sarcasm was not lost upon Rudge even at that
distance, '. . . I *was* beginning to get a little . . .
bored, shall I say? But your recent reluctance
to appreciate my attentions has led me to the
one possible conclusion—that you have found
yourself another lover. Such is my nature—
and by all means call it warped or sadistic or
anything else you choose—that I find a little
competition stimulating. And now, dear girl,
it is your turn to be equally frank with me.
Who is he? Someone I know?'

Rudge felt sickened. He was also deeply
puzzled. How could a woman like Cilla
Newman tolerate the position she seemed to
have got herself into? In what way had she so
put herself in this man's power that he could
lay down the law in such a fashion?

'If I tell you, Philip, will you at least give me
a break?' Her appeal sounded without hope
and Hurst's laugh—cold and merciless—did
not surprise Rudge or, presumably, Cilla.

'You know that answer, Cilla. Besides, I *am*
giving you a break. I can't think of many
lovers . . .' his tone was derisive . . . 'who
would allow you the latitude I do. After all,
I'm not forbidding you to associate with my
successor, am I? I think I'm being quite
outstandingly tolerant.'

'I hate you! I hate you!' It was almost a sob
and once again, Rudge found himself sorry

for Cilla in spite of his predominant feeling of revolt. If he did nothing else at all, he must see if there were not some way he could disentangle Bill Wells from such a woman. Bill was a decent ordinary likeable chap—the very reverse of the type to become involved in this kind of set-up.

'I'm not all that fond of you, my dear!' Hurst's voice was relentless and now definitely sadistic. 'But nevertheless, I continue to find you attractive and as long as I do, I shall expect you to come here.'

'And if I refuse?'

Rudge held his breath. From his summing up, this was the sixty-four dollar question.

'You know that answer, too!' came back Hurst's reply. 'And don't think I won't go through with it. I've nothing to lose. I'm innocent and no one could prove otherwise. But you, my dear . . .'

He left the remainder of the sentence unspoken. Rudge felt the palms of his hands sweating and excitement was coursing through every nerve in his body. Now at last he really was on to something. Hurst was blackmailing Cilla Newman—knew her guilty of something she wished hidden. But what? Was it merely some sexual indiscretion? Or was it something to do with his Mystery Man?

The two voices had ceased. Rudge decided to make his departure whilst he still had the opportunity. He needed time to think before he, himself, made any move. This certainly wasn't the moment for him to call on Hurst for an interview. In fact, he doubted very much whether any point would be served in going to see the man at all now. If he did know anything, he wasn't going to reveal any facts whilst his silence bought him what he wanted. A man like that only talked when it suited him. Money? Rudge rejected the idea. From everything he had heard, it was Cilla Newman Hurst wanted as the price of his silence.

Rudge found himself all but running along the path in his haste to put distance between himself and all that he had overheard in the last half hour. He steadied himself down to a more normal pace and once or twice shook his head as if to clear his brain of the disgust and revulsion left there by the scene he should never have heard. Once again, he almost found himself wishing he had not played spy. But gradually his reporter's sense of excitement overcame all other emotions. He still had no proof but he was more than ever convinced now that he was on to something. If it had been any other woman in Hurst's cottage, he would not have placed so much importance on what was said, but Cilla was the one woman who was, however remotely, connected with the accident at Baker's Pool. Cilla Newman . . .

Suddenly, Rudge halted dead in his tracks.

He swallowed twice, trying to slow the sudden racing of his heart as her name rang a confused message in his brain. Cilla Newman ... Newman ... Frank Newman ... his editor ... the man who had so surprisingly forbidden him from looking into the story for fear of the mud it could stir up.

'Frank Newman!' Rudge said aloud. 'Cilla's brother-in-law!'

He began to move forward slowly, unaware of his surroundings. He was shaken to find himself suddenly upon the edge of Baker's Pool, where only the other day he had stood with Sandie. It looked even more ominous in the grey misty morning light; the water was dank, green, stagnant—a horrible place to die. *Was* it possible Cilla Newman had pushed the Mystery Man in? Not even here, in this horribly gloomy place, could he really believe it. She was of light build, too—physically unable unless she had taken the man unawares. No! He still couldn't believe it.

Rudge climbed the rocky bank in a sudden desire to hurry away from here. At any moment, Cilla might return and she would recognise his car parked on the roadside. For the time being, he didn't wish to have to reveal what he knew, or even that he'd seen her here.

He passed her car half a mile further up the road, turned into a farm lane. He'd not noticed it when he drove by earlier. It was well concealed without obviously being so. Anyone who did see it would probably think she was buying eggs, for a large sign indicated they were on sale at the farm.

Lost in thought, Rudge was almost at Sandie's flat before he realised where, instinctively, he was going with his news. He slowed down, feeling instantly deflated and at the same time, irritated. Sandie would be at school and he could hardly wait for her return at lunchtime since that child, Julia, was no doubt still at her flat.

For a moment he toyed with the idea of going down to the school gates and waiting for the lunch break which would occur at any moment now. He could always send a passing child in to tell her he was there. But he knew as soon as the idea struck that he wasn't going to do that. Sandie hadn't the slightest interest in his story—or in him. She was concerned only with Julia.

He decided to drop by the office—just in case anything had come in he ought to deal with. He'd rung through earlier to say he wasn't too well and would be taking the day off. There was no reason why he shouldn't suddenly have felt better if he ran into Newman.

But Newman had also taken the day off. Betty, the young sub-editress who ran the children's page and some of the women's features, grinned at Rudge in her usual

162

friendly fashion.

'Dead as a dodo in here,' she reported. 'If I were you I'd go home and finish your day off being ill in comfort.'

Rudge had forgotten his hangover but now, suddenly, he was aware of his aching head. He badly needed a drink. He took Betty's advice and repaired to The Waterman's Arms. There, a large log fire burned unexpectedly and most welcoming, in the hearth. Mrs Haycock brought him a plate of veal and ham pie to enjoy with his beer. With this inside him, he began rapidly to feel better. With the renewed energy of body came a renewal of energy of his brain. It teemed with speculations about Philip Hurst and Cilla.

How to find out what Philip Hurst had obviously found out about Cilla? That was what Rudge wanted to know. He rejected at once as hopeless the idea of confronting Cilla with the facts and asking her to explain herself. He'd be an utter fool to think she'd admit to anything. He couldn't even prove she was having an affair with Hurst. It would be his word—his story of what he had overheard—against her denial and although he had not the slightest intention of telling anyone, not even the threat of doing so was likely to frighten her into a confession as to why Hurst was blackmailing her.

What *would* frighten her? Rudge asked himself as he pushed aside his empty plate

163

and started on bread and cheese. Could he bluff her somehow by letting her think he knew all the answers? Somehow he didn't think she'd bluff that easy. If he couldn't buy information from Hurst or bluff Cilla, how was he ever going to discover the facts? Maybe he could persuade Cilla to tell him of her own free will? It would be no bluff if he told her he knew Hurst was blackmailing her. She obviously wished to be free of the man. He, Rudge, could offer to help her get free of him. The law was never on the side of blackmailers and perhaps Cilla did not know that if she were only trying to hide an adulterous association, the courts would keep her identity secret so that she had nothing to fear from Philip should he end up talking. But if, as he himself strongly suspected, Cilla had been in some way involved in the murder at Baker's Pool, if murder it was, then she'd never risk Philip's revealing what he knew.

Tirelessly, Rudge let the questions and answers chase one another round his mind. There had to be a way to get at the truth. If only he could think of it . . .

Quite suddenly, with the arrival of his coffee, Rudge found a possible course of action. He wouldn't tackle Cilla Newman at all. He'd try a more devious route—a route taking him to his own backyard—to the office—to Frank Newman. *He* was in this in some way, too. Rudge was certain of it. He

164

would tell his editor that he was prepared to be sacked but that he was continuing with his coverage of the Mystery Man story because he had now come upon some really salient clues.

At the very least, Rudge told himself, Newman would be worried and as even the most unsophisticated thriller reader knew, a worried man could be panicked into ill advised action; be made to betray himself—or others.

TWELVE

'You'll have to get rid of him,' Gerald kept repeating to his brother with a blustering insistence that annoyed his companion to the point of exasperation.

'How many more times, Gerald, do I have to remind you that I haven't any *grounds* for sacking Rudgely.' Frank Newman stubbed out a cigarette irritably and looked at his brother's perspiring face with a mixture of pity and annoyance. Gerald was such a fool! He had always been a fool and he, Frank, since early boyhood, had had to help Gerald out of the messes he'd got himself into. Over the years it had become second nature to him to shoulder Gerald's problems; try to solve them for him.

But it hadn't been possible even to think of the last problem in the category of 'one of

Gerald's scrapes'. It was far too serious. For the first time in his life, Frank had shied away from becoming involved. But Gerald's whole career—the complete structure of his life—was in the balance and Frank had been unable to remain detached, uninvolved. He would have become involved in any event by virtue of his relationship to Gerald and Cilla.

For several months the three of them had lived on the edge of a precipice; waiting each day for the worst to happen. Then gradually, they had begun to relax and for the past few years, had begun to forget the whole miserable affair. There had been, of course, a few unfortunate reminders. A man in Gerald's prominent position inevitably laid himself open to blackmail if he had anything to hide. But when the decision to pay up had been made—it had been the *only* way to stop the threatened scandal—to behave as if nothing at all had happened.

Now Gerald said:

'It's too risky leaving a chap like Rudgely nosing into the past. I know what reporters are like once they think they are on to something. I don't mind admitting it, Frank, I'm scared. Damned scared! Surely you can find some pretext for firing him?'

Frank Newman ordered two more brandies. Not until they had been put before them did he reply. His tone of voice was a good deal more confident than he felt.

'I don't think Rudgely will pursue the matter further. As I said earlier, I warned him that I wouldn't allow him to go against my explicit orders to leave the story alone. And with the threat of losing his job if he persisted, I threw in a few words about his eventually taking the paper over from me if he played ball.'

'But you said he refused to promise anything,' Gerald reminded his older brother.

'I know. But you are thinking from the standpoint of someone who knows the truth. He does not. *There aren't any leads for Rudgely to follow up, Gerald.* That's what we've got to remember. There isn't a single clue that can point a finger at you . . .'

'What about Philip Hurst?'

Frank Newman's face twisted in a sudden grimace. His voice was filled with loathing as he replied:

'He won't bite the hand that feeds him. Rudgely won't get a word out of him. Frankly, Gerald, I'm much more concerned about Cilla. For one thing, she drinks too much. It can lead to an unguarded tongue. Another point is the reputation she's building up for herself in the district. You've got to take her in hand, Gerald. It's important that people like Rudgely see her as beyond reproach even if she is not,' he added bitterly.

Gerald looked sullen and resentful.

'You know she doesn't pay attention to

anything I say. We had another stinking row this morning because she didn't come home till the early hours. God knows who she was with this time. You know I can't control her.'

'Then it's high time you learned how, Gerald. Use threats if you have to.'

Gerald gulped down some brandy. He looked abject and full of self-pity—far from the upright, dignified Member of Parliament the inhabitants of Ashwyck were supposed to vote for in the next election.

'Don't you think I've tried threats? She just laughs—tells me I wouldn't dare expose her because of what it would do to me and my career. And the devil of it is, Frank, she's right. I'm bluffing and she knows it. Can't *you* talk to her? She listens to you. Can't you make her see that with Rudgely nosing around, she *must* behave herself?'

Frank Newman decided to change his tactics. He'd asked Gerald to lunch with him in order to warn him about the possible risks involved now Rudgely was raking up the old embers. He'd felt it advisable to put Gerald on his guard. Now he saw that he had only succeeded in panicking him. Gerald was so hopelessly weak. He went to pieces in any kind of crisis and Frank didn't want him nervous and uncontrolled. He said soothingly:

'I dare say we're worrying about something which will never happen, so calm down, Gerald. You've got to keep a level head. We all have. We're in this far too deep to be able to afford a false move. Tell Cilla I said so. If you can find a way to warn Hurst, let him know, too. Rudgely will soon lose interest if nothing new turns up to revive his suspicions. It wouldn't be a bad idea for you to take Cilla away on holiday for a while.'

'You know I can't get away now,' Gerald argued, the combination of the second brandy and Frank's calmness beginning to take effect and giving him back some courage. 'With the elections only a few months off, I have to be here.'

Frank Newman studied his brother's face with misgivings.

'You're quite sure you really want to stand, Gerald? You *could* retire from politics. I've thought about this quite a bit and apart from the moral issues involved, it has occurred to me that your position could become even more precarious.'

'Give up politics?' Gerald finally found his voice. 'You must be crazy, Frank. It's my life. Besides, what else could I do? And what do you mean, precarious?'

'You know as well as I do what an election involves—your private life as well as your public record on scrutiny to the public. People have a right to probe. The other parties will try to take up anything they can to discredit you. You only got in by the skin of your teeth last time—and that mainly because this is a totally Conservative seat. The people weren't voting for you, Gerald, so much as voting against the Labour man. And what is your record since?'

'I've not done anything wrong!' Gerald burst out childishly.

Frank sighed.

'You haven't done anything, full stop. The most I've ever been able to give you by way of a boost in my paper is a picture of you opening some damned fête or visiting an old people's home. The country's becoming a great deal more politically minded these days, Gerald. Even in Ashwyck.'

'I've not had any complaints from the Party,' Gerald defended himself, not altogether truthfully. He had, in fact, had several raps over the knuckles for non-attendance at the House.

'Well, you're old enough to make your own decisions about your career,' Frank said wryly. 'I'm only trying to point out that your private life won't stand too much scrutiny, Gerald. For a man not in the public eye, a scandal is serious enough. For you, it would be the end of everything.'

'And you think I don't know that?'

Frank sighed again.

'I suppose so. I wish to God you'd never married that woman, Gerald. I warned you but you wouldn't listen. But for her, we wouldn't be in this hopeless position.'

'How was I to know it would turn out like this? I had no reason in those days to listen to your warnings. You hadn't anything concrete against her then. I admit you said she was hard, scheming, ambitious, but I thought you were just jealous. After all, you never got a wife of your own, did you, Frank?' he added spitefully. 'The girl you wanted turned you down.'

It was so long ago now, the jibe no longer had power to hurt. Frank felt nothing but exasperation and pity as he looked at his younger brother's face.

'It's probably just as well I never did marry—considering what has happened subsequently,' he said quietly. 'Just as well for you, too, Gerald. If I'd married Susan, I might not have been so willing to involve myself in the whole wretched business. I'd have had to put my wife first. Susan wasn't like Cilla—she was decent, good. She'd never have countenanced what we did that night; and I would have deceived her by keeping the truth from her. So count yourself lucky, Gerald, that she married someone else.'

Gerald had the grace to look shamefaced. He owed a very great deal to Frank—everything, in fact, that he had. But for Frank . . .

He shivered, remembering that terrible cold December evening with the rain slanting down and soaking them all to the skin as they stood there listening to Cilla, stunned, shocked, unable for a time to believe the evidence of their eyes and ears.

He gulped down the last of his brandy and would have ordered a third but Frank shook his head.

'Don't be a fool, Gerald. Too much alcohol loosens the tongue and blunts the senses. You need to keep your wits about you. Remember that. I *think* I can keep Rudgely under control but I can't be sure. So you can't afford to take any risks. You understand?'

Gerald nodded. He knew Frank was right. Frank always was right and he had to admit it, even though he resented his brother's superiority bitterly. In Frank's company he had always to face his own weakness of character and for this, he hated his brother even whilst he relied upon him and knew he couldn't manage without him. That very dependence made him doubly resentful.

Gerald returned home in little better frame of mind than he had left after Frank's summons. Cilla, so the cook informed him, had gone up to the Golf Club and would be staying there for the afternoon. Gerald went to his study and tried to do some work but he could not concentrate. Frank had successfully put the wind up him. Now he was no longer completely sure he should pursue his political career. It *could* be dangerous to do so. But then, what had he to fear from exposure if his career collapsed? That was all he cared about. He had no other interests; no other hobbies;

nothing else in the world he cared about. As a Member of Parliament, he was *somebody*: he meant something which not even his wife's scorn or dislike could belittle. She would, of course, leave him if he lost his prominence in society. But he wouldn't care whether she went or not. He no longer loved her; no longer even liked her. In fact, their dislike was mutual. As to making a living, he had adequate private means. But of what use was money once the meaning to his life had gone? It was the respect and kudos his position gave him that was all important.

No! he decided positively. Not even Frank was going to scare him now. Rudgely couldn't be all that dangerous. Frank himself had said there were no clues; nothing whatever to connect any of them with that horrible accident. It was all long ago now. At the time it happened was the time to admit fear, not now. He would have resigned then—wanted to do so. It was Frank who had made him stick it out—showed him that any such move at that time would cast suspicion upon them unless he could find a totally genuine reason for his resignation. He was in robust health. No doctor would have proclaimed him ill. There *was* no valid excuse.

Looking back, Gerald could see that all along they had been forced to act as they had. There had been no alternative. The truth would have ruined them all and so

173

concealment was the only way out.

So deep in thought was he, Gerald did not hear the front door bell ring. He was not aware he had a visitor until the maid knocked on his study door and informed him that a Mr Robert Rudgely was asking to see him.

Gerald was so shocked by the coincidence of Rudgely's appearance at the moment his mind was so filled with apprehension about him, that it was several moments before he could think clearly.

'Tell him I'm out!' he managed to say at last.

'I can't very well do that, sir. He asked if you were in and I told him you were. I didn't realise . . .'

'Very well. Show him into the drawing room,' Gerald broke in irritably. He needed time to calm down, steady his nerves, consider how he would deal with the fellow.

He kept Rudge waiting a full five minutes. When he finally joined him in the drawing room, he had fortified himself with a third brandy. His mood was aggressive. He ignored Rudge's greeting and said curtly:

'I'm a busy man, Rudgely. Unless it is important, I really haven't time to waste with you now.'

Rudge's eyebrows went up.

'Perhaps you won't think what I have to talk over with you is a "waste of time", Mr Newman. It concerns your wife.'

The warmth of the brandy was replaced by a sudden cold shiver down Gerald's spine. To hide his expression, he walked away from Rudge and stood staring out through the French windows into the garden, trying to steady the trembling of his hands.

'I haven't the slightest intention of discussing my wife—or anything else—with you, Rudgely. If you have a statement of some sort to make, then make it and go. But I warn you in advance that I won't tolerate any impertinence from you.'

Rudge felt a moment of pity for the man. He was a fool—but not at this moment entirely without some kind of dignity in his efforts to protect Cilla. Yet his very words indicated his fear that what Rudge had to say was derogatory rather than complimentary.

'I'll be as brief as possible, Mr Newman. You know already that I have been investigating the peculiar accident that happened three years ago at Baker's Pool . . .'

He got no further before Gerald interrupted him.

'And I know also that my brother, your *boss*, Rudgely, has told you to mind your own business. He ordered you to drop the story.'

Rudge felt a swift thrill of excitement course through him at Gerald's unguarded outburst. The fact that Gerald knew his brother had warned him off this investigation further endorsed his own belief that the brothers were somehow jointly involved. Of what interest could Rudge's curiosity about the past be to Gerald otherwise?

'Yes, Mr Newman, I'm aware your brother wants me to drop the story. The reasons he gave me were that he saw no purpose in stirring up mud from the past when it could lead nowhere. But I'm afraid I cannot agree with him. I'm so sure this was no ordinary accident, I'm prepared to take the risk of losing my job on the paper if I have to. I have a hunch, Mr Newman . . . a hunch that someone in this town got away with murder and is possibly walking around at this moment congratulating himself on the fact. I'm sure that you, as a public servant, will back me in my desire to bring the truth to light, if it is possible to do so?'

The young reporter's words filled Gerald's mind with a desperate dismay. If he were indeed uninvolved, he would have no reasons to put the fellow off the scent . . . if he could. Either way now, he would be in difficulties. To encourage him was to lay himself open to every kind of trouble and danger. To discourage him would be to double his suspicions.

'If my brother told you to drop the story, it's because he is convinced that there is nothing more to be unearthed than came out at the inquest. Take my advice, Rudgely, and don't risk your future chasing straws.'

Pleased with the calm sensible tone of voice he had been able to muster, Gerald walked back across the room and stood by the fireplace looking down at Rudgely with a carefully assumed confidence. He was quite unprepared for Rudge's shock tactics.

'Your wife is being blackmailed by Philip Hurst!' he said quietly, his eyes never leaving Gerald's face. The older man's colour drained slowly away. Rudge felt a renewed moment of pity. It was some minutes before Gerald found his voice which had lost all its earlier confidence and was blustering once more.

'That is a slanderous remark, Rudgely. I can only presume that you *think* you can substantiate it but I warn you that I'll take instant legal action against you if you so much as repeat one word against my wife again.'

Rudge took out a packet of cigarettes, lit one and inhaled twice before he said quietly:

'I don't think you fully understand my position, Mr Newman. I'm not out to make a scandal for anyone. What people do with their private lives is their own affair provided they don't harm anyone else in the process. If your wife has been . . . indiscreet, shall we say? . . . that is for you and for her to concern yourselves about. I'm not interested. What does interest me, though, is the crime of blackmail—that ought never to be allowed to go unchecked. And in this case, the blackmailer himself interests me because he

177

was one of the few possible suspects in the case.'

As Newman remained silent, he went on: 'I've come to see you this afternoon because I hoped you might be able to give me an explanation. I discovered that Hurst was blackmailing your wife by accident but I know that it is a fact. There seemed to me to be two possibilities—that you knew already and in order to protect Mrs Newman, were keeping silent for her sake; or that you didn't know, in which case you would undoubtedly want to extricate her from the terrible position she is in.'

Frantically Gerald tried to think how he could cope with this new and threatening development. He wished desperately that Frank were here to advise him. If he only had time . . . he must deny any such knowledge instantly if he were to deny it at all. A man couldn't prevaricate over such a matter. Should he admit he knew? Which would be less damaging? He knew Rudge was not bluffing. The quiet steady matter-of-fact voice convinced him all too soundly that Rudgely had somehow got at the truth—although heaven alone knew how!

'Do you seriously expect me to tell you that all you say is anything but a load of rubbish? Even if it were true, would any man admit it? You'd have to give me proof, Rudgely, before I'd take such a ridiculous idea in the least seriously.'

'I know what I'm saying is the truth, Mr Newman. It's up to you now whether you choose to trust me or not. I don't wish to go to the police with the information I have but you must realise that I have no alternative . . . unless you can give me some kind of explanation. It never has been my desire to ruin people's reputations just to get a good story. Though it may surprise you, I do have my own strange moral code in this respect. But blackmail . . . that is something which should never be allowed to flourish. You must know that as well as I do.'

'And if I don't . . . *can't* give you an explanation, you'll go to the police?'

'I could have gone straight to them,' Rudge said softly. 'I came to you first because I felt you should have the chance to put things right yourself. You know the law as well as I do. If your wife is being blackmailed, you can report it to the police and have the case dealt with so that your wife stays anonymous. I know that in a small village like this, it might prove difficult but it has been done in the past. Why *haven't* you gone to the police, Mr Newman? Exactly what is it that your wife has to hide that she will pay any price . . . Philip Hurst's price . . . to keep his mouth shut?'

Gerald drew a deep breath and let it go on a long deep sigh.

'I haven't been to the police, Rudgely,

because, though this may surprise you, I wasn't aware Hurst *was* blackmailing my wife. Believe that or not as you choose, I swear before God it is the truth.'

The silence that fell between them was broken only by Rudge's faint gasp. It eased the tension between them—a tension that held for one long minute of time while the two men stared into one another's eyes. Then Rudge said softly:

'Strangely enough, I do believe you. But you must admit your reactions are not those of a man in the least surprised to learn such a terrible fact.'

Gerald's face crumpled into a sickly smile.

'Perhaps not, Rudgely, but then you don't happen to have a wife like mine!'

Newman felt a sudden moment of respite. If he could convince Rudgely that Hurst was holding knowledge of a past affair over Cilla's head, there was just a chance the young man would let things be. There was still hope that the whole wretched story would not have to come out. Rudgely had said he had no desire to stir up mud—ruin reputations needlessly—for the sake of a story. So long as the reporter didn't pursue the real reason why Hurst was exacting payments from Cilla—and for the moment he wasn't prepared to think about what kind of payments those might be—they could yet extricate themselves from total disaster. If Cilla's reputation went by the board, it was surely better than the truth.

'My wife,' he said quietly, 'is by way of being a nymphomaniac. I tell you this because I think you are a man of your word. You must realise what it would do to my career if her behaviour came to light. For pity's sake, Rudgely, don't force me to expose her.'

Rudge twisted uncomfortably in his chair. There was something thoroughly objectionable in having to sit and listen to this man plead abjectly for pity. If it were just the Newmans' reputation involved, he'd drop the whole story like a red hot poker. But there was still Hurst.

'You can't sit back and leave a man like Hurst loose on the community,' he said. 'Don't you see, Mr Newman, that a skunk like him could equally be capable of murder?'

'No!' Gerald broke in quickly. 'The police gave him the most thorough investigation. He was in the clear. Take my word for it, he wasn't involved.'

'How can you be sure? They may not have been able to prove he was involved but was he able to produce an alibi? He lived nearer than anyone else to Baker's Pool—alone.'

'But he had no motive. No one but a madman kills for fun and Hurst is sane enough if a little eccentric'

'Eccentric!' Rudgely echoed. 'He's forcing his attentions on your wife, Mr Newman, and you call him "a little eccentric"!'

Something of the scorn in Rudgely's voice

stung Gerald where it hurt.

'So he's a filthy piece of work, Rudgely, but that doesn't make him a murderer. And moreover, why talk at all of murder? It was an accident—nothing more. Why must you keep harping back all those years? What good can it do? The body was never identified. No one missed the man. He can't have been important to anyone. What does it matter how or why he died? Why can't you leave it alone? Even if you're right and someone did kill him, perhaps we're better off without degenerate foreigners like him in this world. That type invariably comes to a sticky end. So let sleeping dogs lie, Rudgely. I'll deal with Hurst, I give you my word. Will that satisfy you?'

Rudgely remained silent. No matter how much he might wish compassionately to put this man's mind at rest, he knew that he could not reply in the affirmative. For Gerald's last few words had convinced him more certainly than ever that his hunch about the accident was right and that somehow all the Newmans were involved.

THIRTEEN

It was only with the greatest difficulty that Sandie managed to concentrate during the morning lessons. No matter how hard she tried, she could not stop her mind returning continually to the same subject—Rudge.

As the morning drew on, Sandie felt more and more depressed. She told herself that if she couldn't give her full attention to her pupils, the very least she could do was to think about poor Julia tucked up in her flat awaiting a visit from the social worker. 'If they will only let me stay with you I can bear anything!' had been Julia's pathetic farewell when Sandie left for school.

But morning had brought an entirely new and contrary desire in Sandie. Gone was last night's irritation with Rudge. Gone, too, was her determination to keep Julia with her. She still wanted to help the girl as much as ever but not at the cost of her own happiness and somehow Julia had become a barrier between her and Rudge.

Sandie despised herself for being so weak. She felt that if she were truly altruistic, she would not now be considering her own feelings at all. She should put Julia first, before anything. But she could not. Rudge kept coming to the forefront of her mind and with him, the quite unexpected fear that he would go out of her life altogether. What had seemed yesterday to be a little more than a rift, today seemed to be the beginning of the end of everything between them. And she didn't want it to end. Fight against it though she might, the fact remained she loved him . . .

In the mid-morning break, Sandie had a new temptation to fight—a weak longing to use the school telephone to ring Rudge and tell him she was sorry; that she wanted to see him; put things right between them. Only now, she wasn't sure if Rudge still cared! She felt depressed enough to believe that he would be fully justified if he had completely lost all patience with her and any love he might have had for her.

Her own, so-newly realised dependence upon him, frightened her. If this was what love was like, she wasn't at all sure she welcomed it. But at least she had discovered one thing—that when she had spoken of love to Rudge before, she hadn't understood the full meaning of the word. Today, on the point of losing him—if she hadn't already lost him—she had suddenly realised just how important he was to her happiness.

'I don't understand!' she told herself miserably. What trick had Fate played that one moment she was only playing at love and the next as deeply involved as any heroine in any romantic book. She had so often despised the weakness of such women, willing to give up anything, subjugate themselves completely, allow themselves to become hopelessly dependent upon a man. How silly they had seemed! How different she, herself, had intended to be. Not for her the old-fashioned idea that a man was a superior being. There was to be total equality in all things. She still believed it in her mind—but her heart was being tortuously betrayed into the admission that she needed Rudge—needed his love, his company, his presence. A life without him had lost all purpose—just as keeping Julia with her had suddenly ceased to have any real significance.

By lunchtime Sandie was ready to admit defeat. But on the point of walking to the telephone, all pride gone in the urgency of her desire to speak to Rudge, she was waylaid by the boy, Tony Dodd.

'Could I speak to you, Miss White? It's important.'

Sandie stared at the boy's pale, taut face and with difficulty recalled that this was the eighteen-year-old with whom Julia had been so friendly.

'I was about to make a phone call,' she began but the boy broke in saying shyly:

'It's awfully urgent, Miss!'

Sandie bit back a sigh and led the way to the now empty art room. She had barely closed the door behind her before the boy broke into a torrent of words.

'It's about Julia. I went to her home last night and her Dad told me . . . about the baby. He kept on and on about it. It was awful, Miss. He said terrible things about Julia and I know they aren't true. I love her, Miss. I know she couldn't be like he said. At first I didn't believe him—about the baby, I mean—but later her Mum said it was true. She told me what had really happened.'

'I'm sorry!' Sandie said gently. 'It must have been a terrible shock, hearing it like that.'

'It was, it was!' the boy said, his large dark eyes never leaving Sandie's face. 'But I didn't think about that then—I just wanted to see Julia only her Mum wouldn't let me; said it was best if I gave her up. She didn't tell me Julia's run away but in the middle of it all, the note came from you saying Julia was at your place. You've got to let me see her, Miss. If I don't see her, she'll think I think badly of her . . . the way her Dad does and I couldn't bear that. I don't care what she's done. It wasn't her fault. Julia isn't a bad girl. She isn't, Miss White. I know she isn't!'

He was nearly in tears. Sandie put a hand on his arm steadyingly.

'I know, Tony, and I think it's very nice indeed of you to stand by her. It'll make all the difference to her to know you haven't lost your belief in her. But . . . well, do you really think it's a good idea for you to see her? It might upset you both and . . . well, there's the future to think of now.'

'You mean the baby!' the boy broke in bluntly. 'Well, I've thought and thought about it all last night and it doesn't make any difference to the way I feel about her. That's all there is to it.'

Sandie was touched—so much so that she felt near to tears herself. Plenty of people had plenty of derogatory things to say about the young but here was positive proof of a genuine loyalty, a capacity for love that was greater than a lot of adults could profess to feel.

'It isn't really quite so simple, Tony,' she said as gently as she could. 'You may be ready to stand by Julia, but you have to remember, it isn't your baby. Besides, you're only eighteen and Julia is only fifteen. You can't think of marriage yet, either of you. You must know that.'

'No, I don't know it,' the boy said, his mouth suddenly set in a stubborn determination. 'I would marry her only my Mum and Dad say the same as you—we're too young. We talked it all over last night. Mum said it wouldn't be fair to Julia because she wouldn't be able rightly to judge her own feelings at the moment. Mum and Dad both know how I feel about *her*. I've loved her ever since I was sixteen and I'll never change. But it's her they're thinking about.'

'Well, that's very nice and sensible of them,' Sandie agreed. 'Do they think you should go on seeing her, then?'

'They're willing for her to come and live with us,' Tony said, the colour now flooding into his face and his eyes bright and eager. 'They know her own parents have turned her out and they think it's awful as I do. They've known her as long as I have, Miss, and she's always been like a sort of daughter to them, them not having a girl themselves. They love her, too, Miss. That's why I've come to you. I know Julia respects what you say. You can make her understand how much we want her. She mightn't believe me. She might think we just feel sorry for her and it isn't that at all. We really do want her.'

He stopped for breath. As the rush of words ceased abruptly, Sandie was forced to turn her head away to hide her threatening tears. Only a few hours ago she had been so completely overcome with pity for Julia—yet now she realised she need not really pity her at all. There were three people in the world who loved and wanted her—in spite of her 'disgrace'. And with a boy like Tony around whom one day she would undoubtedly marry, that 'disgrace' would eventually assume its rightful unimportance.

'You'll tell her, Miss? Tell her we really want her?'

Sandie nodded.

'Of course. And Tony, if I may, I'd like to repeat everything you've said to the social worker who really has far more responsibility than I with regard to Julia's future. I think she will want to call on your parents and talk to them before anything is said to Julia. Do you think that would be all right?'

'We'll do anything you think best,' Tony said in a firm steady voice. 'Mum said to talk to you and do what you say. She's heard such a lot about you from Julia . . . nice things, I mean. She knows you'd only act in Julia's best interests.'

'Thank you, Tony!' Once again Sandie was deeply touched. Her work as a teacher was often tiring, exacting, at times even disappointing. But at moments such as this, all her hard work and enthusiasm and faith in herself were justified.

It was only when the boy left her, her promise to keep him fully informed as to what was happening in his ears, that Sandie had time to appreciate the full significance of the Dodds' offer to give Julia a home. It released her from the necessity to have Julia with her. And with the realisation came an overwhelming sense of relief. She hadn't really wanted to take on such a responsibility. Julia needed parents—not a substitute mother who wasn't even able to run her own personal life in an adult way! How could she have expected to guide and advise and help Julia when she knew so few of the answers to life herself. Maybe Rudge had realised it; that this was what he had been trying to tell her only she'd prejudged him and made up her mind he was just being selfish. Moreover, why should she think it unreasonable of him to put himself and her before Julia's needs? Julia wasn't his responsibility—she wasn't even his pupil. Her own talk of 'humanitarian grounds' now seemed pompous and ridiculous. Of course people had a duty to help one another but not at *any* cost to themselves. There had to be a borderline drawn somewhere as Rudge had seen. If she gave Julia a home, why not Julia's baby, too, and why not any other young girl in trouble until her life was filled with dependent human beings!

She longed even more than before to be able to talk to Rudge now, to explain how she felt. But first she must see Mrs Sinclair who could pass on Tony's message to the social worker. She glanced at her watch and saw that the morning break was nearly over. There wouldn't be time to phone Rudge now, she realised. It would have to wait until lunchtime.

But at lunchtime the girl on the switchboard informed her that Rudge had been in and gone out again and she didn't have any idea where he had gone, or when he would be back. Sandie had to face the afternoon still unable to talk to him and miserably aware that it might already be too late to bridge the yawning gap that lay between them.

When, some hours later, she saw his battered old car parked outside her flat, her only feeling was one of intense relief. She forgot that she had been hurrying home to poor Julia; forgot about Tony Dodd; forgot even that she was due to join a meeting with the headmistress and the social worker in an hour's time.

Rudge was out of the car before Sandie reached the door and he took her in his arms.

'I thought you'd never come!' he said, holding her as tightly as he could. 'I've been waiting for hours. Oh, darling . . .'

He held her away from him so that he could look down at her face. Although she was smiling, he could see tears glistening in her eyes.

'Let's get into the car!' he said gruffly.

He helped her into the passenger seat and closed the door.

'I'd ask you up to the flat . . . but Julia is still there,' Sandie said regretfully. 'Oh, Rudge, I'm *so* sorry!'

Rudge was still too full of joy that their stupid quarrel was somehow miraculously ended to question why she was sorry. It was enough for him that she was here beside him, soft, sweet, utterly feminine and perfectly happy to return his kisses.

'I love you!' he said when at last they broke apart, only their hands remaining tightly clasped to show how unwilling they each were to relinquish contact with one another. 'You're headstrong, and stubborn, and far too independent but I love you. So now you know, darling. I can't fight you. My capitulation is complete!'

Sandie found her voice. It emerged shaky and tremulous.

'That's what I wanted to say to you, Rudge—that *I'd* given in. I don't want to be independent. I just want to be with you!'

They sat silently for a long moment, each a little breathless with surprise and happiness. Then Sandie said softly:

'I think I was fighting against falling in love with you. I suppose I knew that when it happened, I'd be as helpless as any woman in love. I wanted to be able to keep my own identity, Rudge—not to have to become a part of you. But it happened in spite of me.'

'You don't have to fight me, Sandie. I want you to be happy. If you want to keep Julia, that's okay by me, too. I was being selfish—I wanted you all to myself. Today something very important happened—something special and exciting and my first thought was, "I must tell Sandie!" Then I remembered I'd decided I wouldn't see you again until you'd come to your senses and got rid of that poor girl. I sat in the car and thought about it and suddenly I knew nothing that happened was of any importance if I couldn't share it with you. All I was doing by cutting myself off from you was cutting off my nose to spite my face. The fact is, Sandie, I need you,' he added with a self-conscious grin that turned her heart over.

'I need you, too!' she whispered. 'It really

was the same for me—I found out that doing what I wanted in spite of you wasn't bringing me any happiness at all.'

'We've been a couple of fools, haven't we?' Rudge said. 'We've both been used to having our own way and it'll probably take time to learn that doing what you want isn't important when you're in love.'

'Darling, I'm not having Julia after all. I think the Dodds are going to have her to live with them. I've got to go to a meeting soon and it's all going to be discussed. I made up my mind this afternoon that I wouldn't offer to keep her with me unless there really was no alternative. I tried to ring you earlier to tell you, but you weren't there.'

'And I tried to ring you!' Rudge admitted laughing. 'When I got back from the Newmans I phoned the school but they said you'd left. So you see, there must be something in telepathy between lovers after all. Never thought I'd believe that!'

'And I never thought I'd have so little pride as to ring up a man who'd walked out on me! We're learning fast, aren't we, Rudge?'

'I didn't really walk out on you,' Rudge corrected her. 'You sent me packing, remember?'

'I was in a temper because you wouldn't see things my way. Darling, I don't know why you put up with me. I think I'm a very selfish person. I ought to have thought of your side

193

of the question. I did later on, of course. It was only natural you'd be hurt thinking I was putting Julia first.'

'You can't call putting that poor kid first a selfish motive,' Rudge said gently. 'I realised it when I cooled down. It was really typical of you wanting to help any way you could. I should have supported you instead of behaving like a spoilt child myself.'

Sandie snuggled closer against his shoulder.

'I wonder if we'll often quarrel like this,' she said dreamily. 'And make it up like this.'

'I expect we will,' Rudge admitted, stroking her soft hair. 'You can't care very deeply about another person and not get hurt and upset occasionally—at least, not to my way of thinking. I expect even the best marriages have their ups and downs.'

'I want you to know, Rudge, that I'm willing to give up my job if you want me to.'

To Sandie's surprise, Rudge laughed.

'No, darling, of course I don't—not unless you want it that way yourself. Perhaps when we have kids, it'll be different, but you love teaching, don't you? Why should you give it up because we're getting married?'

Sandie drew a long, deep sigh.

'You really don't mind? I was afraid . . .'

'That I was going to be too possessive? No, darling, I want you the way you are, I'm not marrying a housekeeper—I'm marrying Sandie White, with all that goes with her. At

194

least, I hope I am. And bear it in mind, darling, that you're marrying a career man, too. You'll have to put up with my neglect when I'm on a story.'

Sandie gave a mock frown.

'And I know what *that* means—you and your Mystery Man. Rudge, you said earlier that something very exciting had happened. Is it to do with that? I'd almost forgotten about it. That shows you what a bad wife I'm going to be.' She glanced down at her watch and gasped. 'And an equally bad teacher, too. If I don't get a move on, I'm going to be late. Darling, I *am* sorry, but I can't get out of it now. You do understand?'

Rudge sighed.

'Unfortunately, yes! I'll just have to possess my soul in patience. I'll tell you everything after your wretched meeting. Will it help if I drive you there? Where will it be?'

'At the social services,' Sandie said. 'I hope it'll all be over in an hour at the most.'

'Then we'll go out to dinner afterwards— that is, if you can leave Julia. Could you, darling?'

'I'll ask Mrs Dodd if she'll go and sit with her. I'm sure she will. Or Tony. I wanted to tell you about him. He . . .'

'You're going to be late for your meeting, remember?' Rudge broke in.

Sandie stayed long enough for another long kiss before she hurried up to the flat to change her clothes and tell Julia she had nothing to worry about—everything was going to be all right. She longed to tell her about Tony but held back the information just in case the meeting did not go as she hoped. She could imagine Julia's disappointment if it did not.

Julia seemed quieter and more relaxed. Sandie had left her with her own easel and oil paints and the child was contentedly occupied daubing colours onto a canvas. The colour had come back into her cheeks and she seemed quite happy to leave all the decisions as to her future to Sandie. At all events, she was not tense with worry and Sandie realised that the painting was, as she had hoped, proving therapeutic.

'And what about Ma and Pa Forbes?' Rudge asked as he drove Sandie down to the social services. 'Haven't they even visited the girl?'

'No! But they will be at the meeting. Mrs Sinclair said that after discussions with the Dodds, the social worker would talk to Julia's parents and see if everyone could reach agreement. I don't think the Forbes will make difficulties. The father will do anything to be rid of Julia.'

As they were already at the social services office, there was no chance for Rudge to talk to Sandie about his affairs. He opted to wait in the car whilst she was at the meeting and used the time to try to sort out his ideas about the Newmans. Now that he and Sandie were together again, he could give a much clearer concentration to the problem.

When he had left Gerald Newman, Gerald had all but begged for twenty-four hours grace in which to think things over and, indeed, talk things over with his wife. Both he and Rudge knew that it lay within Rudge's power to take his story to the police but neither had brought the subject forward, Gerald because he was afraid Rudge would promptly call his bluff if he challenged him to do his worst; Rudge because he had a hunch he might get nearer the ultimate truth if he waited. He still did not have any clue to connect the Newmans with the accident. Although he was now pretty certain there was a connection, he could not prove it and he wanted proof before he went to the police or, come to that, to his editor, Frank Newman. Once he had all the facts . . . But what were the facts?

When Sandie rejoined him in the car, relaxed and happy now that Julia's future had been more or less definitely resolved and she was to go to the Dodds, she was able to forget the child and give her attention to Rudge. As they drove slowly to the Waterman's Arms, he brought her up to date with the facts. Sandie listened silently, at first shocked by what Rudge told her he'd seen and heard at

197

Keeper's Cottage and then, on second thoughts, not in the least surprised to hear Cilla Newman was involved in such a way.

'Call it a woman's instinct if you like, darling,' she said to Rudge as they settled themselves down at their usual table in a quiet corner away from the bar, 'but I never did like or trust her. All the same, she doesn't seem a likely candidate to be blackmailed, does she? Although I can envisage her doing the blackmailing. Whatever it is Hurst is holding over her head must be pretty serious.'

'Her husband implied it was a past affair,' Rudge interpolated. Sandie shook her head.

'I don't believe that for one minute. Don't tell me he hasn't known for years the kind of woman she is. I'll bet she's had more than *one* affair and he must have known about them.'

'I don't think Hurst was threatening to tell Gerald. The implication was that he could ruin her reputation in the eyes of the public. The impression I got from Gerald was that he did not know what was going on but because his own reputation could be tarnished by Cilla's, he turned a very blind eye. After all, Newman is a public figure, Sandie.'

Sandie sipped her Dubonnet thoughtfully. After a moment she said:

'I don't think any husband knowing his wife was being blackmailed—and in such a way, too—could remain silent about it. In the first place, Gerald could have gone to Hurst and called his bluff—told him to do his worst. If Hurst had climbed down, well and good. If not, Gerald had only to get to the police before him and he'd have had the law on his side all the way. It isn't against the law for a woman to commit adultery—or at least, it isn't a criminal offence. Blackmailing is.'

'Maybe the man's a coward—unwilling to risk his future to protect his wife. But I haven't told you the most important thing of all, Sandie.'

He leant forward on the table, his eyes bright with excitement, like a small boy no longer able to contain the secret he had been bottling up for hours.

'Just before I left Newman,' he said slowly and carefully so that Sandie should not misunderstand a word, 'he did his utmost to convince me that there was no story to be had from the accident at Baker's Pool; that Hurst was not in any way involved and that even if I were right and the Mystery Man *had* been murdered and it *wasn't* an accident, it wasn't important. Then he used these words, Sandie. He said, quote: "Perhaps we're better off without degenerate foreigners like him in this world."'

Sandie frowned.

'Well, perhaps we are at that, though I don't agree it could ever be right not to expose a murder if there had been one.'

'That isn't the important point. It's what he

said about the man being "a foreigner". After I left Newman, I went back over all my notes. Not one word came out in the police reports about the man's identity, his name, his *nationality*. Don't you see, Sandie, how desperately important this could be? How did Gerald know he was a foreigner?'

Sandie's eyes had widened to two large pools of blue.

'Yes, I do!' she breathed the words. 'Anyone *not* knowing differently would have assumed the man was English—or British. It never crossed *my* mind he might be a foreigner. But perhaps there was something on his person, a label on his clothes . . . ?'

'Absolutely nothing!' Rudge interrupted triumphantly. 'His clothes were British made from a chain store in England. Otherwise, the police had nothing whatever to go on. So you see, it was reasonable to assume the man was British. *So why did Gerald Newman call him a foreigner?*'

Sandie sat back in her chair, her eyes half closed now in thought. 'I want to try and think of a plausible answer,' she muttered. 'Not because I don't share your suspicion, darling, but because I do. But I want to see if there *is* an alternative explanation. Suppose . . . suppose Gerald is one of those people hopelessly prejudiced against foreigners. Just because he'd done something bad, Gerald might have assumed . . .'

'Darling, as far as anyone knows, my Mystery Man never did anything bad. He was totally unknown to everyone.'

'So bang goes that theory!' Sandie admitted. 'Then suppose he was dark-eyed, dark-skinned and *looked* like a foreigner? After all, one is inclined to judge people by appearances.'

Again Rudge interrupted with a shake of the head.

'He had blue eyes and "pale" complexion. Admittedly he had dark brown hair but then so have millions of perfectly good Englishmen.'

'And what did Gerald say when you pointed it out to him?'

'I didn't!' Rudge said shortly. 'I don't know why not—perhaps because it was a second or two before I realised what his words implied and then I was too excited to believe my own ears. I thought it best to leave him then. My one thought was to tell you and see what your reactions were. That's when I remembered that we weren't on speaking terms and I nearly died! That was the moment, darling, when I think I realised just how much you had come to mean to me.'

Sandie laughed and screwed her mouth into a mock pout.

'A sounding block! That's all I mean to you!'

'No darling!' Rudge replied seriously.

'That's part of it, of course—the wanting to share everything with you. But what really counted at that moment was that I suddenly realised if I lost you, I wouldn't even care about Gerald Newman or the accident or the story—or anything. I always believed my career was important to me but next to you, it had no real importance at all.'

Sandie nodded.

'That's exactly how I felt—about my teaching,' she said. 'It has always come first—until now. From now on, you come first, Rudge. That's not just the way I want it—it's the way it is whether I want it or not!'

'Do you know, darling,' Rudge said happily, 'that I'd even drop this story if you asked me to. That's how much in love with you I am!'

Sandie laughed.

'And I'd just like to see your face if I asked you to drop it now—at this moment when it really seems you're on the brink of the truth.'

'Yes, I'm sure that I am,' Rudge said, serious once again. 'But how to fall over the brink? Who will reveal the truth? Cilla Hurst? Gerald? Maybe even my boss? I'm sure he's in on this. I never did fully accept his explanations about the missing pages in the paper's files. He's Gerald's brother—obviously he'd protect him as far as he could. But how far, Sandie? Could Cilla have murdered that man? And if so, why? And if not, why is Hurst blackmailing her? Someone can answer these questions. But who?'

'Not me, darling,' Sandie said regretfully. 'I have to get back and give Julia some supper. Mrs Dodd is coming in to sit with her later so I'll be back; but as I've left the child alone all day, I can't neglect her any longer.'

'No, of course not. I'll drive you back and meet you at the Waterman's Arms later.'

'About seven-thirty?' Sandie suggested.

Her conscience nagged her as they drove home. Poor Julia had had a long, lonely day, she reflected, and she ought to have gone straight back after the meeting.

But she need not have worried. A flushed, starry-eyed figure hurled itself into her arms as she opened the door.

'Oh, Miss White, Miss! You can't guess what's happened. I'm so happy. I've been longing and longing to tell you.'

Sandie looked at the girl's radiant face and drew her down to the settee.

'Now tell me all about it,' she said.

Suddenly shy, Julia held out her hand and pushed several crumpled sheets of paper into Sandie's lap.

'You read it,' she said breathlessly. 'I want you to. It's private really but I want you to see. I know *you'll* understand. It's from Tony!'

It was a young boy's first love letter to his girl. In a way, Sandie felt guilty at reading something obviously meant only for Julia's eyes, yet at the same time, she could understand the girl's desire to share it.

Nobody could ever make me believe what happened was your fault, Julia, so you're not to worry about it because it can't alter the way I feel about you. I know the kind of girl you really are—my kind of girl and the girl I want to marry.

I don't suppose they'll let us get married perhaps for years but I want you to know I want to marry you if you want to marry me. I know what Mum and Dad say is true and that we're both still kids really but growing up won't change how I feel about you because I've always loved you ever since I first saw you that day in school.

Mum and Dad are going to try and persuade your parents to let you come and live with us. If you can it'll be sort of like having a sister around the place but I'd rather have you here as a sister than be worrying about where you are and if you're well and happy and that kind of thing.

I'm not supposed to tell you about it until after it's all decided but I want you to know that I want it and hope you want it too. If I don't mind about the baby you shouldn't mind either because I want to love everything about you, even your baby, so you can keep it if you want to. I expect there will be talk at school but I'll be leaving soon and so will you and anyway, I don't care what people say because I only care about you. Please find a way to write back to me and say that this is the way you feel, too.

From your loving Tony

Sandie handed the letter back silently. When she could trust her voice, she said:

'I think you're very lucky to have someone love you like that. Tony's a nice boy, Julia.'

'I think he's wonderful!' Julia cried. 'Oh, Miss White, do you think they *will* let me go and live with Tony's mum and dad? They're ever so nice. Do you think Dad will let me? Oh . . .'

She broke off, clapping her hand to her mouth, the colour rushing to her cheeks.

'What's the matter, Julia?' Sandie asked.

'Oh, Miss White whatever must you be thinking of me. I mean you offering to have me here and me being so ungrateful.'

'Don't give it another thought, Julia!' Sandie broke in smiling. 'Of course I don't mind—in fact I'll let *you* into a secret since you've confided in me—I'm hoping to get married very soon. So you see, it'll be quite useful having the flat to ourselves!'

Speaking of her forthcoming marriage aloud to Julia had the effect of bringing it much closer. While Julia chattered on excitedly, Sandie sat back trying to imagine sharing her little home with Rudge; having him come home at night, waking up in the mornings with him; going to sleep at night with him; watching him hang new curtains or fix a new washer on the kitchen tap. Suddenly, it was all imminent . . . and wonderfully exciting. She thought of Rudge awaiting her return in The Waterman's Arms and firmly ejected the chattering girl while she went to her own room to make herself more beautiful for Rudge.

'You'll be all right here by yourself until Mrs Dodd comes?' she asked feeling guilty again and yet impatient to be back with Rudge.

Julia nodded and after hugging her, urged her on her way.

'I know what I feel like when I'm going to meet Tony,' she said, no longer a child but as woman to woman, understanding about love.

FOURTEEN

Cilla Newman sat alone in the near empty Club House toying with her fourth brandy, an ashtray filled with cigarette stubs on the table in front of her. Her nerves were strung so tightly that not even the steady intake of alcohol she had consumed through the long afternoon had succeeded in relaxing her.

She was perfectly aware that she needed all her wits about her and too many brandies would take the keen edge off her mind. If only she could make up her mind! So far, she had seen Bill only for a brief minute or two when he had returned to the Pro's shop between lessons. The presence of another woman awaiting a lesson had made any kind of private conversation impossible. Bill had been very offhand. He looked pale, tired and was obviously suffering from a severe hangover. She had tried to console herself with the thought that this might well account for his coolness.

Unfortunately she was not scheduled for a lesson. Without glancing at his appointment diary, Bill had informed her that he was booked up all afternoon and could not fit her in.

'See you later, then, at the Club House. I'll stand you a hair of the dog,' she had said but there had been no answering smile and Bill had turned away to talk to his waiting pupil.

But Cilla was not to be left in doubt as to whether or not Bill was intentionally offhand. Screwed up in the ashtray in front of her lay a note the barman had given her round about tea-time.

Sorry I won't be able to have that drink— have previous engagement for this evening. Bill.

Cilla's first reaction had been one of anger but this soon gave way to a vicious determination not to let Bill Wells off the hook too easily. He'd spent the best part of last night with her and he owed her some consideration.

But no one knew better than she did herself that a polite 'consideration' from Bill wouldn't be enough to satisfy her. A pretence that the occasion had meant more to him than a mistaken drunken orgy might give her a chance to salve her pride but she wasn't interested in saving face—she wanted Bill. It was a very long while since she had wanted any man the way she had wanted him.

In the early hours of the morning, as she had driven herself home, Cilla had been fairly confident that the night was the start of a serious affair between them. She realised that he had had far too much to drink and was only barely conscious of what he was doing, or even of who she was, but she counted on him remembering enough to convince him he wanted more of her. That was the way she felt about him and she'd taken it for granted he'd feel the same way.

Entirely without morals, and without scruples, Cilla failed to take into account that Bill might be of a very different ilk. Now, trying to see through his eyes, she was forced to remember that bachelor though he was, she was a married woman. There was, too, the question of their ages. Although Cilla knew she was still a very attractive woman, she was no longer a girl to attract Bill with her youth and beauty. The last time she had been with Philip Hurst he had cruelly pointed this out to her. How she hated that man! She'd thought that if she were able to get free of him, she would be perfectly happy. But now she knew better. She wanted to be free of Philip because she wanted Bill, and it certainly didn't look as if she were going to get him.

The question now was how to handle the situation. If she left the Club House, accepting Bill's note as if she believed he had a previous engagement, he might think she was going to take his rebuff lying down. On the other hand, she could not afford to have a showdown with him in the Pro's shop if she cornered him there on his return from his last lesson. Bill was popular with men and women alike and people walked in and out continuously. There was equally no point in waiting here for she was sure now that he would not come in this evening for fear of running into her.

There were, of course, very few places Bill could go of an evening in Ashwyck—The Waterman's Arms, or back to his cottage. Unless, of course, he really *did* have a previous engangement and someone had invited him out to dinner at their house . . .

Cilla was far from sure how she would tackle Bill even if she did run him to earth. But because it was what she wanted to believe, she half managed to convince herself that Bill was behaving in this way because he was afraid to have an affair with her. It could lose him his job if they were indiscreet and people found out and talked. This morning he may have thought it over and decided she wasn't worth the risk! But if she could see him, talk to him, persuade him otherwise . . .

Hardened to heavy drinking though she was, Cilla was far from sober when she finished her fifth brandy and made up her mind to go to The Waterman's Arms. If Bill did not turn up there by seven o'clock, she would drive over to his cottage. But she was not going home until she had seen him . . .

She had left the Golf Club only a matter of minutes before Gerald telephoned to ask her to come home at once. She would not necessarily have gone home if the message had reached her before she left. But the very strangeness of his phoning her at all might just have warned her that something very important must have happened to make him break the now long-standing rule that they each go their own way without interference from the other.

Happily ignorant of the cloud hanging over her head, with only the thought of Bill in her mind, Cilla parked her car in the yard outside The Waterman's Arms.

As usual, the pub was full. It was some minutes before Cilla caught sight of Rudge sitting alone at a table by the window. She turned her head away quickly, not wishing to become involved with him but he had already seen her and came across to the bar where she now stood.

'Won't you join me at my table?' he asked.

Cilla hesitated. It must have been obvious to him that she was alone. If she told him she was waiting for friends, and he continued to sit here all evening, he would see that she was lying if Bill should not come in.

'Well, for a moment or two . . .' she said vaguely and allowed Rudge to guide her back through the crowd to his table.

'Were you waiting for somebody?' Rudge asked innocently. He wondered if she had a rendezvous arranged with Bill and remembered that he had resolved to have a word with the poor chap, warning him off before he became too involved. Not that Rudge would ever normally dream of poking his nose into another chap's affairs but this was different—Bill was an easy-going, good-natured Australian bordering on the naïve. He'd probably never come across a woman like Cilla Newman before and certainly would not suspect what she was capable of. And what was she capable of? Rudge asked himself wryly. Murder?

'You weren't at home when I called this afternoon!'

His words dropped into the silence that

followed his last unanswered question. Cilla's face swung round to his, suddenly alert.

'You were at home? To see Gerald? Or me? Why?'

The staccato questions gave away her uneasiness. Rudge could almost feel her fear as if it were a tangible object.

'I went to see him about Philip Hurst,' he said quietly, watching her face. A little too quickly, she dropped her eyes. Rudge saw that her hands were trembling as she reached into her handbag for a packet of cigarettes.

'Oh, about that crazy idea of yours that Philip Hurst had something to do with the accident?' she said when she had lit up. Her voice was now fairly well under control.

Rudge felt the excitement of pure tension inside him. He decided on the spur of the moment to use shock tactics. They sometimes worked and he had nothing to lose. She had obviously not yet been home, so Gerald could not have put her on her guard.

'I went to see your husband after I discovered Hurst was blackmailing you. I wanted to know why neither you nor your husband had been to the police!'

Cilla, tensed and wary though she was, was unable to prevent the gasp of surprise, dismay, fear that escaped her lips. The hand holding her cigarette trembled so violently, she stubbed it out quickly.

'What did Gerald say?'

212

Rudge continued to watch Cilla's face closely.

'He didn't deny it. He couldn't very well since I was absolutely sure of my facts.'

Cilla was aghast. She was out of her depth now and did not know what to say. She fell back on anger as her only possible way of gaining time.

'Exactly what has my private life to do with you? You've no right to pry into my life—or Gerald's. What is it you want anyway? Money?'

Rudge controlled his anger with difficulty.

'Oh, no, Mrs Newman. *I* am not a blackmailer. I am interested only in the truth. And I still have not found out what the truth is. Strangely enough perhaps, I don't think you are the kind of woman to sit down under blackmail—not unless you had something far more drastic than a mere love affair to hide. What exactly *are* you hiding, Mrs Newman?'

Fear was now the only emotion in her body. Cilla fought against it but one quick glance at Rudge's face showed that this time she was not going to be able to bluff her way out. Tentatively she said:

'You're a reporter, Mr Rudgely. If I did have something to hide, I'd be the world's prize fool to tell you of all people, wouldn't I?'

'Perhaps! Perhaps not. I'll get at the truth eventually so it's only a matter of time. Even you must realise that now. If it should turn out that you are really an innocent victim of circumstances, then I might be on your side. But you'd have to prove your innocence, Mrs Newman, and that means you wouldn't get away with a fabricated story. I want the truth.'

'You're bluffing!' Cilla said, too panicky now to think coherently. 'You don't really have anything on me. You're trying to make me talk. I don't believe you know anything.'

'Would you like me to list the facts I have?' Rudge asked ruthlessly. 'They don't look too good when you add them up. One, I know Hurst is blackmailing you. Two, I know your husband is a party to it. Three, I know that the man drowned in Baker's Pool was a foreigner and that the circumstances in which he died were highly suspicious. Four, I know that your brother-in-law tried to protect someone by removing all published accounts of the accident from the newspaper files. Five, I know that he did his utmost to stop my investigation into the accident, just as you and your husband tried to put me off. It doesn't need much more, even you will admit, to make it obvious Frank Newman has been trying to protect you or your husband and that all three of you are sufficiently afraid of exposure to permit blackmail of the worst possible kind. So now *you* tell *me*, Mrs Newman, just what is the connection between you, Hurst and the dead man whom only your husband knew was a foreigner. Did *you* kill him? And if so, why?'

Before Cilla could answer, Rudge felt a tap on his shoulder. Looking up, he saw Sandie. She could hardly have chosen a worse moment to arrive. She was nodding to Cilla and innocently sitting down in the vacant chair beside him. Rudge could find nothing to say. Cilla, too, was silent.

'Am I interrupting something?' Sandie broke into the silence. 'If so, I can easily go and wait in the car.' She looked at Rudge anxiously but it was Cilla Newman who replied.

'I was about to suggest that Mr Rudgely came home with me for a drink. You see, I have something to tell him. It's a long story and this is hardly the place to tell it. I suppose since he'll eventually tell you anyway, it doesn't really matter a damn if you come, too. Shall we go?'

Sandie felt Rudge's hand on her arm. The fierceness of his grip revealed his tension. Some of his excitement passed to her. It wasn't until she was alone with Rudge in his car, the red reflectors of Cilla's Jaguar lighting the road in front of them, that she was able to question him.

'I think this is it!' Rudge said in reply. 'I don't know what happened before she came into the pub but I caught our Mrs Newman with her guard down. I was lucky, I suppose, that she hadn't been home and talked to

Gerald. He might have put her on her guard. They could have cooked up a story, maybe . . . enough to keep me at bay a little longer. Now I think she knows it's too late for that.'

Sandie shivered.

'In a way I'm sorry for her, Rudge. It must be terrible to have done something so awful that you'll do absolutely anything to avoid being found out. Do you *really* think she killed that man? If she did, it means she is capable of murder and what she did once, she could do again. Suppose she tried to kill you, darling, to keep you quiet? Me, too. I think I'm scared!'

For the first time in the last hour, Rudge laughed.

'You've been seeing too many television thrillers,' he told her. 'You can't just bump people off, put your gun away and sit back saying "that's that!" There'd be our two bodies to dispose of, remember? She can hardly throw us both into Baker's Pool. No, I doubt very much Cilla Newman is a murderer in your meaning of the word. But I am absolutely convinced that somehow or other she was involved in the death of my Mystery Man. Now I believe we're going to be told how and why.'

Ten minutes later Rudge and Sandie were sitting side by side on the elegant sofa in the Newmans' drawing room. Gerald stood alone at the far end of the room, his face averted, looking old and drawn. Cilla sat in a chair opposite her guests, pale-faced but upright as if determined to cling to the last remnants of her pride.

'It isn't a very nice story,' she said, glancing briefly at Sandie as if aware that she was going to shock the younger girl. 'But it's the truth, for what it's worth. When you've heard it, you can ruin Gerald and me if you choose. Just now Gerald tried to stop me talking but what's the use when it's obvious you're going to find out everything anyway.'

'I still think Frank should be here . . .' Gerald burst out but Cilla broke in with a cruel laugh:

'And how's your precious brother going to help us this time, Gerald? Don't be such a fool. Our luck ran out the day Rudgely, by some wretched quirk of Fate, started raking up the past. Looking back, I suppose we could call ourselves lucky that no one before him wanted to probe deeper into the cause of Pierre's accident.'

Sandie felt Rudge's body stiffen at the sound of that Christian name. She could feel excitement radiating from him like an electric current. The air itself was tense with expectation.

'It's the end of everything!' Gerald spoke dramatically, from behind them.

Cilla lit a fresh cigarette, shrugging her slim shoulders as she blew out a cloud of smoke.

She was remarkably calm.

'Maybe so, Gerald—yet in the last resort what have we to lose, you and I? Our marriage—ruined beyond repair anyway. Your career—and what real happiness has your career brought either of us? Oh, I know the lengths to which we've both gone to preserve it but now suddenly I find myself questioning whether it has proved worth while.'

'It's everything to me!' Gerald stated bluntly.

'And you've always let me know it meant more than I!' Cilla's voice was filled with bitterness. 'But let's have it on record, Gerald, that I paid the bigger price trying to keep your precious name intact. You only paid in cash!'

This time Gerald did not reply. Cilla's head turned away from her husband and back to Rudge.

'I know you must want me to begin at the beginning but I'm not sure what was the beginning,' she said softly. 'I suppose it was the day Pierre came into my life and made me realise how hopelessly empty my marriage had become. Gerald was always away. I was lonely, bored, frustrated. Pierre was younger than I, nice-looking, French, with a Frenchman's way with women. He came from a poor family who considered he'd done very well for himself when he became chauffeur to a wealthy businessman in Paris.'

Cilla drew a deep breath and leant back

against the chair cushions, closing her eyes as if in darkness she could remember better.

'He lost his job when the man suddenly died whilst on a business trip to London. Pierre decided to stay in England and ultimately became part houseman, part chauffeur to us. It wasn't long before I realised that Pierre found me fascinating. From sheer boredom, I allowed an affair to develop.'

'Must you go into these details?' Gerald broke in, his voice rough with embarrassment.

'Yes, I must, if I'm to make our friend here see the truth—the whole truth and nothing but!' Cilla gave a short, bitter laugh. 'You see, Mr Rudgely, I may have behaved immorally but not criminally. I didn't know then that Pierre was a gigolo; that what he was really after was money. I believed he was in love with me. I was very generous to him. For a while I was happy. Then Gerald found out and Pierre was sent packing.'

'I should have divorced you then,' Gerald burst out. 'You were no better than he.'

'But you didn't want a divorce, did you, Gerald? You preferred to swallow your pride and keep me than face the publicity the case would have stirred up. That's when I really understood how things were between us. I rented a flat in London for Pierre and visited him there whenever I could. I suppose this could have gone on for years but

219

unfortunately for Pierre I discovered he was merely using me to support his girlfriend. So I gave him up. There was an ugly scene but Pierre saw I meant it. I gave up the flat and he disappeared. I thought that was the end of the whole sordid business. Pierre had nothing on me since Gerald already knew the facts. I never expected to hear from him again.'

She paused long enough to go to the sideboard and pour herself another brandy. She seemed quite oblivious to the other people in the room. She merely nodded towards the drinks and said 'Help yourselves if you want anything.'

No one moved. Cilla sat down again, holding her glass with both hands, staring down into the tawny golden liquid.

'Several years later, Pierre turned up, down-at-heel, out of work, and begged me for money. The girl he was keeping had turned out no better than he and had walked out on him when she'd soaked him for every penny he'd saved and she knew there was no more coming. Gerald had refused to give Pierre a reference and he'd been unable to get a decent job or settle down to the more menial ones open to him. He said he wanted to go back to France, to make a fresh start in life and had come to me for his fare.'

Cilla's shoulders lifted slightly in a shrug of self-derision.

'Hard to believe, I suppose, but I paid up. I

. . . I'd been fond of him and he spun a good story . . . but he didn't go to France. He went to Scotland and got himself a job way up in the north where his employer didn't bother to check his self-written reference. I wouldn't have known this as I never saw him again until the night he died . . . except that he had a letter on him from his Scottish employer saying Pierre had stolen money from him. It was only then his boss checked up on him and found the reference to be phoney. The letter was to inform Pierre that a week's wages were enclosed in lieu of notice, and why.'

Now Gerald took up the story as if caught up in it despite himself.

'It was no doubt in the hope of another hand-out from Cilla that he came south. He could only have arrived that evening on the day train for he had a Scottish newspaper on him of the same date. We think, being short of cash, he hitched a lift from London down here and got off the car or lorry where the Ashwyck road joins the main road. He was walking towards this house when . . .'

Abruptly Gerald's voice came to a halt. He, in turn, went to the side table and poured himself a large whisky.

Cilla took up the story again.

'It was a terrible night!' she said. 'Pouring with rain and visibility dreadful. Gerald and I had been out to dinner and we'd both had a fair amount to drink—Gerald even more than I.

221

Not that he was drunk—or that the accident was his fault. This shadow just lurched across the road in front of us. No one could have stopped in time. Gerald stamped on the brakes and we skidded across the road a few yards before he could stop the car. We weren't going too fast because of the rain and bad visibility. But we knew we'd hit something—or someone. We felt the bump and saw a shadow catapulting sideways towards the bridge.'

'I got out and walked back to look,' Gerald said. 'I was soaked through in seconds. I still didn't know then who or even what I'd hit. But there was no body on the road—nothing.'

'Gerald came back to the car and asked me if I was sure I'd really seen someone or something,' Cilla broke in. 'We sat there for a minute or two not really sure and yet feeling it was unlikely both of us could have been mistaken. We asked each other if we should just drive on but . . . well, somehow we couldn't do it. It was such a terrible night. No other cars were likely to pass by. It was nearly midnight, you see, and we realised that some poor devil could be lying injured and might even die if we left him.'

'We should have gone on. That was our biggest mistake,' Gerald said as much to himself as to his listeners.

'Well, we didn't,' Cilla said flatly. 'We'd nothing to be afraid of then. We knew it

222

wasn't our fault and if and when we found someone, we were going to take them straight to the Cottage Hospital. The only problem then was finding who we'd hit—if there really had been someone, and we still weren't sure.'

'I got out of the car and started looking again more methodically,' Gerald broke in as Cilla paused. 'I found faint traces of skid marks—the rain was heavy enough to wash most of them away—and located where I thought was the exact spot I'd seen the shadow as it bounced away from the car. I was on the bridge. I don't know what made me look down into Baker's Pool. Logically it was a stupid thing to do because in that weather, in the dark, I couldn't have expected to see anything. But . . . but I did. He was floating face up in the water. It was the whiteness of his face I saw as I flashed my torch over.'

Gerald took a large gulp of whisky and sat down heavily, covering his face with his hands as if he could not bear to relive the nightmare of that moment, all too well remembered.

'I heard Gerald shouting and ran over to the bridge. Then together we went down and half dragged him out on to the rocks.' Controlled though she was compared to her husband, Cilla's voice trembled. Somehow it made the account all the more convincing to her listeners.

'At first we were only concerned with the fact that the man was obviously dead. We

223

didn't know then that he'd drowned. We thought it was the fall or because of some injury he'd sustained when the car hit him— or he hit the car,' Cilla continued. 'Then, as I stood there staring down at him, I thought I recognised him. I simply couldn't believe it for a while. I told myself it was someone who just *looked* like Pierre—his double or something like that. I think I was a bit hysterical by then. Gerald took over and started to search his pockets. That's when we found the letter from Pierre's employer and knew for certain it was him.'

Now that this part of her story was told, Cilla suddenly seemed calmer, as if the rest were somehow unimportant.

'We couldn't decide what to do,' she said. 'Gerald wanted me to help carry him up the bank and put him in the car but the bank was steep and I'd never have been able to lift that dead weight. I hated the thought of touching him. I did try but I lost my hold and he slipped back into the water. We were both sick with horror. Gerald said there was a flask of brandy in the car and we'd go back and drink it and decide what to do.'

'But once away from that ghastly spot we couldn't go back,' Gerald took up the story. 'We still didn't intend to leave him. We were going to go home and ring up the police and let them fish him out. But on the drive home I decided to ring my brother first—he's always been the level-headed, sensible one of our family. I wanted him there when the police came to ask questions.'

'By the time Frank arrived we'd changed into dry clothes and were a bit calmer,' Cilla said, 'Of course we had to tell him the whole story—about Pierre, I mean. It was only when Gerald was actually saying Pierre had once been my lover that I realised what this accident might look like to the police. Suppose they didn't believe it was an accident? Suppose they thought we'd known Pierre was coming to visit us, perhaps to blackmail us or something, and that Gerald had decided to get rid of him? We couldn't *prove* we didn't know he was coming. We couldn't prove our innocence even if the police couldn't prove our guilt. But circumstances could make us look very guilty.'

'Frank thought so, too,' Gerald interpolated. 'And he saw at once that I'd been drinking. By that time I'd had a couple more stiff whiskys to steady my nerves. At the best, Frank said, the police would suspect I had been drunk when driving the car and that wouldn't look too good. At the worst, we could be involved in the most appalling scandal and might even be accused of deliberately murdering the wretched fellow.'

'We stood to lose everything if we informed the police,' Cilla summed up flatly. 'Pierre was dead, we were sure of it. Nothing could help him; nothing at all was to be gained by a confession. We went over the accident again and again. No car had passed us. No one could possibly have seen us. Most important of all, Pierre was not known in Ashwyck since we'd been living in London when we'd employed him, so no one we knew was likely to connect him with us. When his body was found, he'd be an unknown man who'd accidentally drowned himself in Baker's Pool.'

'There was only the matter of any identification papers he might have on him to worry about . . . We decided one of us would have to go back and remove anything suspicious from his pockets.' Gerald said. 'I was pretty drunk by then so Frank came with me. It was still raining. The skid marks had completely gone and there wasn't even a trace where Cilla and I had climbed the bank. Pierre was there, though, still floating . . .'

Without knowing it, Sandie had sought the comfort of Rudge's hand. Now she moved even closer to him, shivering at the mental picture Gerald had evoked.

'That's all there is to it,' Cilla said not without irony in her voice. 'Except, of course, for Philip. God knows what nefarious business had kept him out so late on such a terrible night. He never told me. But he was walking home through the woods when he heard the screech of our car tyres and saw our headlights through the trees. When he heard voices he realised there had been an accident of some kind and walked back to see.' She shivered at the memory. 'He was standing there all the time Gerald and I were trying to get Pierre out of the water; watching us. He could have helped out. He didn't. He just stood there watching to see what we would do.'

'Once we had decided that night not to report the facts, there was no turning back.' Now Gerald's voice was calm, matter-of-fact. 'Early the following morning, a passing cyclist saw Pierre's body and went to the police. It was too late then for us to do or say anything, even if we had wanted to. Our silence during the night was in itself incriminating. So we were committed to going through with our plan to keep quiet about our part in the accident.'

'Thereby giving Hurst his opportunity to blackmail you,' Rudge ended the story for him.

'At first he only wanted money,' Gerald said nodding. 'Then . . . I suppose you despise me for allowing it but Cilla never told me about their affair until it had been going on some time. To have gone to the police at this stage would have been even more incriminating for us as by then I'd already paid out regular sums of money to Hurst as the price of his silence. Would an innocent party have done such a thing? The obvious inference was that we were guilty. We knew we couldn't stand a chance. The facts against us were far too black.'

Glancing at Cilla's face, Sandie was shocked to see how pale and drawn she had become. She seemed to the girl to have aged years in the last half-hour. As if aware of Sandie's scrutiny, Cilla turned and looked towards the couple on the sofa.

'I don't expect you'll believe it, but Gerald didn't kill Pierre that night. Even if he had been completely sober, he couldn't have prevented the accident. *Pierre ran into the car.* I thought about it afterwards and decided he was probably trying to thumb a lift and because he was afraid he wouldn't be noticed in the dark and rain, ran too far out into the road. If he'd been a stranger we'd have gone straight to the police. So you see, it's all my fault we're in this predicament—not Gerald's.'

For the first time since she'd known her, Sandie felt differently towards this woman. Despite everything she was now forced to a reluctant respect. At least Cilla was brave enough—and honest enough—to shoulder the blame. She had made no attempt to whitewash her part in it. In a way, Gerald came out of this the worst of the two.

'So there is your story, Rudgely,' Gerald spoke flatly, without hope. 'Frank won't print it, of course, but every other paper in the

228

country will. Frank warned us that if the truth ever came out we'd have to stand trial. All this time we've had that hanging over our heads. In a way I'm almost glad we've nothing to fear any more.'

Now it was Rudge's turn to help himself to a drink. His thoughts were in turmoil. At last he had the truth—if the Newmans' word could be trusted—and somehow, he didn't doubt every single word was true. The pieces all fitted exactly into place. There were no discrepancies. The Newmans could never have made up and told that story in such a way if it had been pure fiction. Besides, if they had wished to kill the wretched Pierre, there were far less dangerous ways of disposing of him than to run him over almost on their own doorstep.

So it was, after all, an accidental drowning, as the coroner at the inquest had found. Frank Newman had spoken the truth when he'd warned Rudge that to stir up the past would achieve nothing and possibly do great harm. How little Rudge had understood then to what Frank really referred! No wonder his editor had tried so desperately to put him off the story!

On one point Rudge had already made up his mind. He wasn't going to write up the story. But, he asked himself, knowing what he now knew, was it his duty to go to the police? If he did, what good would it serve? The

Newmans were innocent of any crime unless it were that of withholding evidence. To produce that evidence now was to ruin three people's lives needlessly. The only person who really deserved punishment was Hurst.

'Hurst cannot be allowed to get away with the blackmail,' he spoke his thoughts aloud. 'But to expose him is to expose you, too.'

'You mean you aren't going to the police?'

Gerald's mouth hung loose with surprise.

'I don't know,' Rudge said truthfully. 'I just don't know what I ought to do.'

'I'll resign, of course,' Gerald burst out as hope began to kindle within him. 'I realise my career is ended now. It really should have ended that night and I've known it deep down inside. But I will retire—take Cilla right away from Ashwyck—start a new life somewhere abroad perhaps, My God, Rudgely, if you'll give us a chance . . .'

He broke off no longer able to control his voice.

It was Cilla who retained her self-control. She said to Rudge:

'Perhaps if you and I were to go to Philip and tell him Gerald and I have made a full confession to you and intended going to the police, he'd be so afraid of the consequences to himself that he'd get out quick. I think he'd do a disappearing act.'

'And go unpunished?' Rudge said. 'A man like that deserves the worst the laws of this

230

country could give him. Why should he get off scot free—perhaps to start blackmailing someone somewhere else?'

Cilla shrugged.

'He'd never know whether the police were after him or not, would he? That would be a punishment—and a deterrent—and one that would be with him for the rest of his life. He'd never know, would he, if he were on the file of wanted men?'

Rudge was silent. To carry out such a plan was to take the law into his own hands, to mete out justice in place of the law. Would justice be better served *by* the law? The Newmans could well be convicted of murder; Frank Newman as an accessory; and in the light of the truth, this would be a travesty of justice. Was this, after all, what he wanted?

'I need time to think,' he broke the silence at last. 'I'll come and see you both tomorrow morning and let you know what decision I've come to.'

It was after eleven o'clock when Rudge drove Sandie home. They did not once broach the subject so terribly in the forefront of their minds. Sandie did not want to prejudice Rudge's decision by imposing on him her own predominate emotion—that he should be lenient; show pity for the two people caught up in the web of Fate.

FIFTEEN

Two months later Sandie was lying on the beach in the South of France, her head resting against Rudge's suntanned shoulder, her own body golden-browned by the sun, oiled and at rest beside him.

They were on their honeymoon—an ecstatic two weeks of sunshine and love and the beginning of a closeness of mind as well as body that often made conversation between them unnecessary. It was this strange telepathy of lovers that permitted Sandie to guess at Rudge's thoughts now.

'You're thinking of the Newmans, aren't you?' she asked, running a finger gently along the side of his jaw.

He turned his head and lightly kissed the top of her nose. It was faintly freckled. He kissed it again.

'Yes, I was. I was thinking how terrible it must be to be married to someone you didn't love. I don't imagine the Newmans ever loved each other.'

'Perhaps they did—once!' Sandie said sighing. 'I wonder where they are now.'

'Norway, I think,' Rudge replied. 'Gerald Newman has a cousin out there who owns a paper mill. I think Frank told me the cousin had given Gerald a job of some kind. I don't suppose they'll ever come back to England now.'

I wonder if they are happy!' Sandie mused.

'I shouldn't think so. Gerald is too weak a character ever to make anything worthwhile of his life. Even his political life was a sham—a façade. Without Frank behind him, he'd never even have got that far.'

'And Cilla? Was there ever any good in her?'

'Not much! Perhaps a stronger man could have coped with her, managed her. Women like her need strong men.'

'The way I need you?'

They both laughed.

'You know very well I'm as weak as water in your hands, my girl. But for you, I think I'd have turned the lot of them in. You convinced me I shouldn't.'

'I did no such thing!' Sandie sat up and stared down at Rudge indignantly. 'I never said a word to influence you either way.'

'You may not have said much but waves of emotion poured out of you. Don't deny you wanted me to keep my mouth shut and let sleeping dogs lie.'

'Only because it seemed to me they'd been punished enough. And because it would have been on your conscience all your life if they had been wrongfully convicted.'

The smile left Rudge's face.

'I don't know, darling. I have faith in our British justice . . . I think it's very, very rarely we convict innocent people. But I admit that even if they had got off in the end, they'd have had to stand trial first and the publicity would have ruined them for the rest of their lives. All the same, I think I *would* have turned the Newmans in. You see, I couldn't have lived with my conscience, letting a blackmailer like Hurst go scot free.'

'It was extraordinary, wasn't it?' Sandie mused. 'I know he'd apparently had a weak heart for years and could have popped off at any time, yet to have died the very day after the Newmans had confessed . . .'

'Almost as if he'd had a premonition that the game was up,' Rudge agreed. 'But he couldn't have known a thing about it. He was in one of the village shops when he collapsed so there was never any question of foul play. I was on my way to the Newmans' house to tell them I'd made up my mind I must report what they'd told me when I saw the ambulance and heard what had happened. Perhaps it was stupid, but it gave me the strangest feeling . . . as if Fate had deliberately intervened by bumping him off so I would decide after all in favour of the Newmans.'

Sandie nodded understandingly.

'It must be pretty awful for the Newmans, knowing we know the truth and could, at any time, expose them.'

It was some time before Rudge spoke again. When he did his words surprised Sandie.

'You know, darling, once Hurst was dead, the Newmans really weren't in any danger. It was Frank who pointed this out to me. You see, apart from Hurst actually seeing them at Baker's Pool, there was never any proof they'd been near the place at the time of the accident. Pierre was never identified and I very much doubt that after so long, I could have proved that the dead man *was* Pierre. I was the only one who knew Hurst was blackmailing the Newmans or even that Cilla had been visiting Hurst's cottage. So you see, it was just my word against theirs and Gerald was still a very much respected member of the Ashwyck community. Maybe they couldn't have proved their innocence but British law demands that someone else should prove their guilt. Without Hurst, what proof did I have?'

'I heard their confession, too, remember?' Sandie reminded him.

'Yes, darling, but we might have cooked up the whole story between us.'

Sandie frowned impatiently.

'And why should we do such a thing?'

Rudge laughed and pulled her down again beside him.

'A reporter can make a hell of a lot of money out of a story like that. I'd have made a small fortune—and it would have come in very handy since I was about to make you my wife.'

' "Bob Rudgely, brilliant young reporter on *Stanfield Observer* uncovers sordid secret behind mystery drowning at Baker's Pool".'

Rudge grinned.

'Yes, and it would have hit the headlines, Gerald being who he was at the time. So you see, my dearest and nearest, we had a motive for creating such a story and the Newmans had no proven motive for the crime. So if you'd been a member of the jury, you'd have said no case to answer!'

'So that's that!' Sandie said conclusively. 'And next time, my nearest and dearest. . .' she laughed as she echoed his words . . . 'that you have a hunch to follow a story and I have a hunch that you should leave it alone, I trust you'll listen to me.'

'No woman,' said Rudge firmly, 'however beautiful, however gorgeous, however desirable, is going to dictate policy to the new editor of the *Stanfield Observer*. Understand?'

'Oh dear!' said Sandie with an exaggerated sigh. 'And I thought I'd married Bob Rudgely, reporter!'

'No, darling,' replied Rudge kissing her. 'You married a strong man.'